THE WHITESTONE STORIES

THE WHITESTONE STORIES

Seven Tales from the Stone Age to the
Bronze Age for the Children (and
Grown-ups) of All Ages

John R. Barrett

with Christine Clerk, Illustrator

iUniverse, Inc.
New York Lincoln Shanghai

The Whitestone Stories

Seven Tales from the Stone Age to the Bronze Age for the Children (and Grown-ups) of All Ages

iUniverse books may be ordered through booksellers or by contacting:

iUniverse
2021 Pine Lake Road, Suite 100
Lincoln, NE 68512
www.iuniverse.com
1-800-Authors (1-800-288-4677)

This is a work of fiction. All of the characters, names, incidents, organizations, and dialogue in this novel are either the products of the author's imagination or are used fictitiously.

Illustrations are by Christine Clerk

John Barrett and Christine Clerk are hereby identified as authors of this work in accordance with the Copyright, Design and Patents Act, 1988

ISBN-13: 978-0-595-42435-1 (pbk)
ISBN-13: 978-0-595-67998-0 (cloth)
ISBN-13: 978-0-595-86770-7 (ebk)
ISBN-10: 0-595-42435-X (pbk)
ISBN-10: 0-595-67998-6 (cloth)
ISBN-10: 0-595-86770-7 (ebk)

Printed in the United States of America

C O N T E N T S

▼

FOREWORD

The Whitestone Stories are the lost myths and memories of long-ago.

In the first age of *The Man and the Forest,* Nature's truths dwelled even in a child's heart—and that is *How the Boy Found His Name.*

Kindness and Strangers laid waste the wildwood, to renew the land in the age of golden corn. But *The Girl Who Made a Friend* did not heed the Whitestone's warnings, and so her wishes all came true.

Pride wrecked the world. But a germ of goodness sailed through the tempest in the silver boat of the Moon, and in *The Making of the King,* the world was remade anew and golden. Wickedness could not prevail against the cunning of kings, and so *The Craftsman's Reward* was strangely gifted by the gods.

At last, when good folks' hearts were fogged by disrespect, *The Girl Who Danced* performed her dance of death. And all was well.

INTRODUCTION

THE WHITESTONE'S STORY

On a gently sloping place among the fields stands a rounded white stone. In Summer the Whitestone is a glimmering pearl set in the gold of the rippling barley. In Winter the Whitestone glisters through the short days when the stubble and ploughed soil are bleak and frozen. The Whitestone quietly watches, through rain and wind, ice and sunshine: patient while the years grow into centuries; untiring while the centuries stretch into millennia. If only she could speak—what tales might the Whitestone tell!

The motherly Whitestone remembers all the times of her life in the world. Dimly she recalls how, in a faraway time, she was born—a plump white egg in the hot belly of the World. She lived long ages in the warm darkness. She was a wordless dream in the orange rocks at the roots of the granite mountains. She blinked, like a new birth, into the light. She lived a while in the sheering winds of a teetering crag. Then she was plucked from the earth. She was gripped in a clasp of frost. She slumbered in a blue embrace of ice that carried her far from where she was made. It placed her here on the hillside where she now stands.

The Whitestone watched while the walls of ice melted. She basked in the sunshine. A mountain-white hare nipped the grasses at her feet. She heard the beat of his fast heart, so fearful though there was nothing to fear. A shy juniper rooted in her shade, growing strong with green life. A bright bird perched upon her shoulder to sing its song of brittle joy. The Whitestone warmed with love for the living things that came to her. She gave them names and called them all her children. The forest drew its cloak of foliage across the hillside. The Whitestone nestled within its whispering silence.

*   *   *   *

10,000 years ago
The hunter-gatherers of the Mesolithic (Middle Stone Age)

In this first age, long long long ago, forest covered the whole land. The wildwood of tall pine trees and spreading oaks was the home of fierce creatures. These included the graceful lynx (a silent hunting cat) and the aurochs (a fierce wild bull). And there were wolves and bears, wild boar and beavers too.

The first people arrived in the wildwood. These forest folk lived by hunting. The men used bows and arrows or long spears. They made traps and nets and snares. They hunted animals to eat; and from the skins and fur the women stitched warm clothing. The tools and weapons of these hunting people were made of stone and wood and bone and antler.

The people of the forest also gathered fruits in the Summer and mushrooms in the Autumn. They dug up tasty roots. And especially they collected hazel nuts, which formed a most important part of their food. Gathering was women's work, though the children helped too. The women were skilled in the use of herbs. They made baskets from bendy willow stems and other containers from the white bark of the birch tree.

The people of this first age were always on the move, searching for animals to hunt and for places where nuts and fruits could be gathered. They did not build houses. They lived in tents covered with animal skins and in shelters made from branches thatched with leaves and grass.

A favourite place to pitch camp was on the seashore. Here the men could hunt seals for their meat and warm fur. The men also went out to sea in their dugout canoes and skin-covered boats to catch fish with hooks and nets and spears. The women and the children gathered bird's eggs (and birds too). They collected crabs and shellfish among the rockpools. In some places we can still see where these hunter-gatherers lived. Today we sometimes find the remains of the hunters' campfires and the flint tools they dropped and lost on their travels. We also see, near the seashore, big rubbish heaps (called middens) with all the discarded shells and bones from their seafood feasts.

*   *   *   *

7000 years ago
The first farmers of the Neolithic (New Stone Age)

Later—but still long long ago—new people arrived. These were the Neolithic folk—people of the New Stone Age. They spoke a different language from that of the hunter-gatherers. They followed a very different way of life. The Neolithic folk were the first farmers.

The Neolithic folk came from beyond the sea in boats. They brought with them new kinds of animals—creatures that the hunter-gatherers had never seen before. These included sheep, goats and small good-natured cattle. Farmers of the New Stone Age used sharp polished axes, made from flint and other hard stones, to cut down the forest. They chopped down the trees and burned the under-growth to make space for gardens and fields. They built sturdy houses of stone and wood. The Neolithic folk also brought with them seeds of wheat and barley which they sowed in their gardens and fields. They harvested the corn, which they ground into flour and made into bread.

The New Stone Age was a time of new things. Women made pottery—which was unknown to the hunter-gatherers. The women also spun and wove the wool from their sheep and goats into cloth. Women were the wise leaders of the community.

On a high place near to each village the farming folk built a great house of stone. And when they died, the people's bones were put into the stone house. Neolithic folk believed that the spirits of the dead would live in the stone house. The ghosts of all the past generations—the spirits of the ancestors—watched over the people and their crops and animals.

Neolithic folk also worshipped the sun and moon that shone on their houses and fields, bringing life and light to their corn, and their cattle—and also to the spirits of the ancestors in their stone house. Big stones—tall, slender father stones and round fat mother stones—were raised among the fields or beside the ancestor house. These friendly giants were worshipped as the fathers and mothers of the whole community

The Neolithic age was a time of sunny skies and warm weather. It was a good time to be a farmer. In due course all the forests were cut down; the land was covered with fields and filled with people. We do not know what happened to the hunter-gatherers. But without the forest to live in there was nothing for them to hunt. Perhaps they learned how to become farmers. Perhaps they were enslaved or killed by the Neolithic folk. Certainly they disappeared from the land.

But then, perhaps because of a change in the weather, things changed. The Neolithic way of life came to an end. The houses of the ancestors were sealed up. A new way of life emerged.

*   *   *   *

5000 years ago
The gods and kings of the Bronze Age

The new way of life may have been brought by new people who arrived from over the sea. Certainly many things changed. In place of the spirits of the ancestors, the people now believed in the power of gods who lived in the sky—in the sun and moon and stars. They worshipped these gods in temples. These were built as circles of great stones, perhaps with a bank and a ditch outside the ring. In some parts of the land long rows of great stones (or small stones) were set up to point to the rising sun and to be a place where the gods could be honoured.

The warm weather returned and the fields again grew crops of wheat and barley. The New people made pottery and wove cloth—though in styles very different to those of the Neolithic folk. They also now used a wonderful new material for their tools and weapons. The people had found out how to make and shape metal. Copper was mined and smelted to make tools and jewellery. Copper was mixed with tin to make bronze. Bronze was harder than copper. Metal axes and knives were sharper than the stone blades of the Neolithic. But metal was rare and difficult to make. Many people could not afford bronze and so they continued to use stone tools.

The leaders of the Bronze-Age communities were men. And these men were kings, whom the ordinary people respected or feared. They thought their kings were specially chosen by the gods. Women were no longer the leaders of the community. The kings possessed fine bronze knives and axes. They wore gold and green-glass ornaments on their clothes and in their hair. The kings also wore broad crescent-shaped collars of jet or amber beads. These rare and beautiful stones were brought by traders from far away, or even from beyond the sea.

When a king died he was buried in the earth. Sometimes the king was buried in a coffin made from a hollowed-out tree trunk. Most kings were laid—curled up as though asleep—in a shallow pit lined with slabs of stone. Over the king's grave was heaped a big mound of earth or rocks. This mound was built on a high place above the fields where it would be seen by everyone. The Bronze-Age people believed that the king went to live with the gods when he died. And so they placed in his grave all the things a king might need for his life in heaven—his knife and axe, his bow and flint-tipped arrows, his jet necklace. The dead king was provided with a joint of meat with a pot of drink (probably beer) to eat during his journey to the heavens.

But then the weather changed. The time of warm sunny Bronze-Age weather came to an end. Our own age of rainy cool weather began. The corn did not grow well and there was much hunger and disease. People began to fight among themselves for the best places to live. Villages became like fortresses, defended by walls and ditches. The people thought that the gods of the sun had hidden from them. They began to worship new gods and goddesses who dwelled in the dank forests and dark pools that began to form across the land.

$$*\qquad *\qquad *\qquad *$$

These are the three first ages of people in the land. Mesolithic hunters, Neolithic farmers and Bronze Age kings all made their homes, lived and died beside the round wise Whitestone. There have been other folk too—people who came later—and who also left their mark upon the land. The Whitestone remains, unchanging through all the changes.

Today the farmer ploughs the field around the Whitestone with a loud tractor. Sometimes he thinks he will come with ropes and chains to drag the stone away. But he never does. He knows the Whitestone belongs in this place. He knows that this place belongs to the Whitestone. He knows she watches over him—her latest child—like a pale strong mother. She watches over his fields. And she loves all the people and all the plants and creatures who live in her world. She is filled with deep thoughts. She remembers all the times of her quiet life.

CHAPTER 1

▼

THE MAN AND THE FOREST

When the Summer came to the forest, the spirits of the trees (who see all things in the wildwood) wrapped the bare branches in heavy cloaks of green. When Summer came to the forest, all the thickets sparkled with red raspberry jewels; and the grasses were spangled with scarlet strawberry drops as bright as the garnets in the mountain rocks. When Summer came to the forest, the tangled underwoods wore emerald fruits upon their brambly fingers and Autumn nuts began to plump on the hazel.

But all was not well in that long long long-ago time. The Spirit of the Earth was troubled. She felt that there was something new in the world. But it was a thing for which she had no name, and so the Earth was troubled. And when the Earth was troubled all the spirits and the creatures of the forest who were her children became uneasy too.

The leaves fluttered anxiously. The tall pines leaned their heads together and the spirits of the trees (who see all things in the wildwood) murmured fretfully.

Small creatures scuttled fearfully among the rustling litter of last year's leaves. They met in their tunnels among the tangled grass to chatter in shrill and frightened voices. The beaver in his strong lodge of logs and sticks made grave speeches to his mate. Then he paddled across the broad pond for serious conversations with his neighbour. The antlered stag and the angry aurochs (the fierce wild bull of the forest) met in a green clearing. They spoke in haughty tones.

And the forest that covered all the land seemed to mutter with one voice, "What can it be? What can it be?"

The troubled Earth went to her sister, the Spirit of the Great Waters. They met at the places where the waves break.

They met at the places where the waves break

"Yes, I have seen it," gurgled the water in the rock-pools. "I have seen this new thing, but I do not know what it is."

"Is it a creature?" asked the Earth.

"Indeed I think it may be so," roared the wave at the foot of the cliff. "But it is not as other creatures. It did not know me as it rode upon my back, and it changes its skin from day to day."

"Can you describe the creature?" asked the Earth.

The sea spoke from the splash of the tide in a sea cave. "I have seen the creature stamp upon the ground in a deerskin coat. But it is not an antlered stag or timid hind. I have seen it dash in the sunshine with a shining skin. But it is not a quick lizard or a glossy frog. I have seen it with an otter's pelt and a spotted cat's skin, but it is none of your forest children."

"How can this be?" mused the Earth. "But tell me dear sister of the sea: from where does the creature come?"

"He comes from far away," whispered the voices of the ocean in the ears of the shells on the shore. "He comes from beyond my far horizon."

"Tell me now," the Earth begged her sister, "how does the creature come so far? Does he fly like the swans who straggle across the Autumn sky, fleeing the cold wind of the North?"

"He does not fly. He cannot fly," swirled the salt spray.

"Then does he swim?" asked the Earth. "Does he live in the body of the deep like the shining salmon who come to leap in the plunging waterfalls of Spring?"

The rattling pebbles of the breaking wave replied, "I have seen him swim. But in the waters he is clumsy like the wild boar when he crosses the wide river. And the new creature travels on the crests of my waves. He is not swift. He swims as heavily as a log of wood or some dead seal."

"Is he a dolphin, or a whale, or a basking shark?"

"No. He is not the joyful porpoise, nor the prowling orca, nor the gaping grey fish. He is not a creature of the sea."

"Does the creature have a name?" asked the Earth. "For I am his mother and must know my children's names."

"It would be better if you had never known this child," hissed the sea-foam on the sand. "Beware my sister, Earth. Beware this latest child. Beware the last creature in the world. Beware the thing whose name is Man."

Then the Earth thanked the Sea. The tide sighed and kissed her sister's hand. She felt sorry that she had allowed the Man to ride upon her back. She was sorry that she had carried the Man from far away to trouble her sister's spirit and her family of the forest.

The Earth was troubled. She called together all the spirits and the creatures of the forest. She called to the spirits of the trees (who see all things in the wild-wood). She called to the sly spirits of the dark places, and to the secret spirits of the stones. She called to the sprites of the laughing waters. She called to the trembling flowers. She called to the sleeping bats and the butterflies of the forest air. She called in a loud voice so that all the slow snails and snakes and busy beetles and slumbering Autumn toadstools of the forest floor might hear. She called to the shy shiny frogs and sticklebacks and the hovering dragonflies of the woodland pools. She called to all her children. And all came to their mother's call. They came to the broad white mothering stone in the heart of the forest. All came except the Man. The Man did not hear—or did not heed—his mother's voice. The Man did not come when the deer and the boar and the fox and the badger and the birds and the angry aurochs (the fierce wild bull of the forest) all came to the Earth's clear call.

... all the spirits and the creatures of the forest

The Earth was troubled. She spoke to her obedient children.

"Hear me," she cried. "There is a new creature in the forest."

Then all of Earth's children—all of the trees and spirits and creatures—were glad. The pine marten and the honeybee laughed together in the treetops. The slowworm and the brown bear were happy. The whole world of the wildwood rejoiced because their mother Earth had a new child.

But the Earth was not joyful.

"I do not know this creature who is called Man," she said. "He is my child because I am the mother of all things that live. But I do not know this Man. And he does not know me. He does not hear—or does not heed—my voice. The Man does not love his mother," said the Earth in a voice of tears.

"There is a new creature in the forest."

Then all the spirits and creatures were dismayed.

"Beware the Man!" cried the Earth. "The Man who does not know—or does not heed—his mother, will not know his brothers and his sisters. He will not love the spirits. He will not respect his fellow creatures. Beware the Man! He will not be your friend."

Up spoke the spirits of the trees (who see all things in the wildwood). "We don't care," they said. "Who can harm us when we flit through the high branches? Who can hurt us when we hide in the sap of the yellow wood beneath the hard bark? We are not afraid of the Man."

... the spirits of the trees

"Oh beware!" cried the Earth. But the playful spirits of the trees (who see all things in the wildwood) had already flown to find the Man and tease him with their tricks.

Then all the creatures and the spirits went their separate ways.

Next day the spirits and the creatures of the forest met together. They met at the broad white mothering stone in the heart of the forest. But the pride of the trees had fallen from them like the leaves in Autumn. Amber tears streaked the red bark of the tall pines. The heart of the oak was split with sorrow and the willows drooped.

"What has happened?" cried the Earth, who was the gentle mother of the trees.

"We have seen the Man," the branches creaked and clashed. "We spoke to him but he did not hear—or would not heed. He tore our bark to bleed our sweet sap. He cut our branches with an axe of flint. He bent our limbs to make his lair. His mate stripped us of our fruit. She left not one ripe hazel nut behind to feed the hungry squirrel or to grow next year into a new green tree. She made a flame that was not lightning from the sky. She made a fire to burn our broken branches all day long—and all night too—upon the forest floor. She sang a song beside her campfire—

It is good to live in the forest. I shall take all that I want.

The Earth was sad and stern. "You were proud, but now you have learned a lesson. You were mischievous, but now you have taught a lesson to your brothers and your sisters." The Earth spoke to all her children. "See how the poor trees are wounded and afraid! Learn the lesson that they teach. Beware the Man."

"I don't care," said the old grey she-wolf. "I am cunning. I am quick. My pack is panting in the thicket. I shall not fear this Man. He shall fear me. I shall grip him in my strong jaws. I shall hold him by the throat until the breath has left him. I am not afraid."

"Oh beware!" cried the Earth. But her daughter, the old grey she-wolf, had already slunk on silent hunting paws into the forest. She had gone to hunt the Man. She would avenge the hurt that had been done to the harmless trees. She would rid the wildwood of the cruel Man.

Next day the spirits and the creatures of the forest met together. They met at the broad white mothering stone in the heart of the forest.

The Earth said, "Where is my daughter, the old grey she-wolf?"

"We do not know," said the spirits of the trees (who see all things in the wildwood). "But today we saw the Man. There was a smile on his face. His mate wears a shaggy wolf-skin coat. And the Man wears four yellow wolf's teeth in a necklace about his throat. There was a wolf cub at his side—a slave to help his hunting. And the Man sang a song beside his campfire—

It is good to live in the forest. I shall take all that I want.

Then the Earth and all the spirits and the creatures of the forest wept for the old grey she-wolf. And when they had finished their weeping, the Earth repeated her warning, "Beware the Man."

"I don't care," said the big brown bear. "I have my sharp claws. I have my strong arms. When the Man comes near I shall catch him. I shall wrap my arms around him. I shall crush the life from him. The Man will learn to fear the big brown bear."

"Oh beware!" cried the Earth. But her son, the big brown bear, had already padded on heavy hunting paws into the forest. He would hunt the Man. He would avenge the hurt that had been done to the harmless trees. He would rid the wildwood of the cruel Man.

Next day the spirits and the creatures of the forest met together. They met at the broad white mothering stone in the heart of the forest.

The Earth said, "Where is my son, the big brown bear?"

"We do not know," said the spirits of the trees (who see all things in the wildwood). "But today we saw the Man. There was a smile on his face. And tonight his cubs are hugged snug in a bearskin rug. And the Man wears a bracelet of brown claws about his wrist. He sang a song beside his campfire—

It is good to live in the forest. I shall take all that I want.

Then the Earth and all the spirits and the creatures of the forest wept for the big brown bear. When they had finished their weeping, the Earth repeated her warning, "Beware the Man."

"I don't care," said the soaring buzzard. "I can fly high on the back of the wind. I can taunt the Man who walks upon the forest floor. I shall teach him to respect his mother. I shall make him cry for the big brown bear and the old grey she-wolf. My mournful voice will make him grieve until he leaves the forest forever."

"Oh beware!" cried the Earth. But the soaring buzzard had already mounted on the broad back of the wind, flying on the keen wings of the air to find the Man. She would avenge the hurt that he had done to the harmless trees. She would rid the wildwood of the cruel Man.

Next day the spirits and the creatures of the forest met together. They met at the broad white mothering stone in the heart of the forest.

The Earth said, "Where is my daughter, the soaring buzzard?"

"We do not know," said the spirits of the trees (who see all things in the wildwood). But today we saw the Man. There was a smile on his face. And he wears on his head a crown of feathers. And the arrows that fly from his bow (flint-tipped as sharp as a wasp) soar on the back of the wind guided by three brown flights from our sister's wing. The Man sang a song by his campfire—

It is good to live in the forest. I shall take all that I want.

Then the Earth and all the spirits and creatures of the forest wept for the soaring buzzard. When they had finished their weeping, the Earth repeated her warning. "Beware the Man."

"I don't care," said the bristling boar. I have my strong back and my tearing tusks. I can rush through the brambly thickets. I can knock the Man down. I can break his bones. I can teach him to hear—and heed too—the voice of our mother. I shall make his mate to weep."

"Oh beware!" cried the Earth. But her son, the bristling boar, had already rushed into the forest. He would avenge the hurt that had been done to the harmless trees. He would rid the forest of the cruel Man.

Next day the spirits and the creatures of the forest met together. They met at the broad white mothering stone in the heart of the forest.

The Earth said, "Where is my son, the bristling boar?"

"We do not know," said the spirits of the trees (who see all things in the wildwood). "But today we saw the Man. There was a smile on his face. And his two cubs each wear a boar's tooth to give them strength. And there is fat pork roasting on his fire. The Man sang a song by his campfire—

It is good to live in the forest. I shall take all that I want.

And there is fat pork roasting on his fire.

Then the Earth and all the spirits and creatures of the forest wept for the bristling boar. When they had finished their weeping, the Earth repeated her warning, "Beware the Man."

"I don't care," said the angry aurochs (the fierce wild bull of the forest). "I have my thick hide which the Man's flint arrows cannot hurt. And with my wide horns I shall toss the man like dust in the air. I shall teach him to hear and heed his mother. I shall make him know the wrong he has done."

"Oh beware!" cried the Earth. But her son, the angry aurochs (the fierce wild bull of the forest) had already trampled on furious hooves into the forest. He would avenge the hurt that had been done to the harmless trees. He would rid the wildwood of the cruel Man.

Next day the spirits and the creatures of the forest met together. They met at the broad white mothering stone in the heart of the forest.

The Earth said, "Where is my son, the angry aurochs (the fierce wild bull of the forest)?"

"We do not know," said the spirits of the trees (who see all things in the wildwood). "But today we saw the Man. There was a smile on his face. And his mate has made a fine new lair and pitched over it a snug dry tent of oiled leather. And the Man calls to his friends far away with a bellowing horn. The Man and his mate and his cubs all sang a song by their campfire—

It is good to live in the forest. We shall take all that we want.

Then the Earth and all the spirits and creatures of the forest wept for the angry aurochs (the fierce wild bull of the forest). When they had finished their weeping, the Earth spoke.

"Now I shall show this cruel Man my anger. He will know the sorrow of a mother who has lost her children. He will know—and all the spirits and the creatures of the forest shall know—the anger of a mother when her children are wilful and do not hear—or will not heed—her wisdom and her warnings."

And all the forest was afraid. The spirits and the creatures of the forest fled to their lairs and burrows. The tall trees bowed their heads. The small flowers closed their petals. All the creatures and the spirits of the forest feared the terrible anger of the Earth.

Now the Earth let loose her rage and sorrow. Her tears of grief for all her lost ones fell as drenching rain. And for her disobedient ones, her tears fell as stinging sleet and hail. The Earth's dismay that her own children did not hear—or would not heed—her words, made clouds of darkness hide the sun by day and all the stars by night. Her song of loud despair was a wailing wind that whipped the grasses and bent the trees.

The spirits and the creatures of the forest shivered in their lairs and burrows. Meanwhile the Man learned to hear—and heed—his mother's voice. The Man's bright campfire was drenched and the damp sticks he cut would not burn. The Man could find no animals to hunt. The Man's shelter of skins and sticks and stout branches, thatched with turf and sedges, dripped with water. And when the storms came, it blew away like thistledown. The Man and his mate and his children were wet and hungry, miserable and cold.

The Man's bright campfire was drenched

At last the motherly anger of the Earth ebbed away until only a weary sadness remained. The Earth was sorry for her children who were cold and frightened. But she was not sorry that her children had been punished for not heeding the words and warnings of their loving mother.

Next day the spirits and the creatures of the forest met together. They all came to the broad white mothering stone in the heart of the forest.

The Earth said, "Where is the Man, my newest child?"

"I am here," said the Man. And he stood with the animals and the spirits.

The Earth looked at her newest child. She saw that the Man was not strong like the bristling boar or the angry aurochs (the fierce wild bull of the forest). But he was cunning like the yellow-eyed fox and patient as the ring-tailed cat. She saw that the Man had no coat of fur to keep him warm like all the animals; no down of feathers like the birds; no thick hide like the angry aurochs (the fierce wild bull of the forest). But the Man could hunt and make fire and build a shelter. The Earth saw that the Man had no sharp claws like the big brown bear, no fangs like the old grey wolf, no clutching talons like the soaring buzzard. But he carried an axe of flint and a knife of flint and a long straight spear with a shaft of ash and a point of flint. He bore a tall stiff bow of yew, and on his back was a quiver of arrows—all finely feathered and barbed with shards of flint.

"And what do you want?" the Earth asked the Man.

"I want the rain to stop so that I can light my fire. I want the winds to cease so that I can rebuild my shelter. I want the sun to shine so that I can hunt. I want to live in the forest and to take all that I want to live."

"I shall make the rain stop so you may light your fire," said the generous Earth. "I shall make the winds cease so you may rebuild your shelter. I shall allow the sun to shine on you and on all my children. But I shall never let you live in the forest and take all that you want."

"But if I cannot live in the forest I shall die," the Man complained. "If I may not take all that I want, my mate and my children will starve. Cruel mother, who would watch her newest children perish!"

"You shall not perish," said the kindly Earth. "Your mate and children will not starve. You will live in peace and plenty forever if you hear—and if you heed—my words."

"Then tell me, mother, I beg you, what you would have me do."

The wise Earth smiled upon her newest child who now could hear—and heed—his mother's voice.

"Love me and love my children. Love all the spirits and the creatures of the forest. Then, though you shall not live *in* the forest, you may (like all my children) live *with* the forest. And, though you shall not take all that you *want*, you may (like all my children) hunt and gather for your family, and be given all that you *need*."

Now at last the Man understood. He understood that the world that was made for him was made for all the spirits and the animals as well. The world was made for him to belong to, not for him to own.

Then the Man and the Earth and all the spirits and the creatures of the forest were filled with joy. And so, during all his long first age, Earth's newest child lived in harmony with the spirits and the creatures of the wildwood. At night the Man and his mate and his children sang a new song beside their campfire:

> *It is good to live with the forest.*
> *The Earth gives all that we need.*

CHAPTER 2

▼

HOW THE BOY
FOUND HIS NAME

In the long long long-ago time there lived a boy. He lived with his father and mother, his sisters and brothers in the forests of the first age of people in the land. He lived in the time when wildwood of tall pines and spreading oaks trees filled all the valleys and covered the plains and the hills, almost to the very mountain tops, in a cloak of green.

In Summer, the boy's mother chose a camping-place in a sunny glade near to a stream of chattering water. She pitched a cosy tent of skins which was the family's home during all the long warm days when the sun was high in the sky.

When Winter came, the boy's father found a dry place sheltered by overhanging rocks or the spreading branches of some ancient tree. Then the boy's father and his big brothers cut branches with their flint axes. They tied them together using the strong roots of the pine trees or ropes plaited from leather and nettle stems. They bent the green branches over. They wove them together. Then the whole family gathered grass, turf and bracken fronds. With these they covered the roof of their Winter house so they would be warm and dry while the days were cold and dark.

The boy liked his Summer home

The boy liked his Summer home beside a great whitestone in the heart of the forest. On warm nights he would lie outside the tent beside the smouldering campfire. He watched the fluttering moths that came to dance near the flames. He watched the bats that came to hunt the moths. He watched the stars that flickered among the tree tops. Now and then a mischievous spirit would stir the fire and a spark would escape, flying upwards to join its crystal sisters in the sky. When it rained, the boy lay awake inside the skin tent. He listened to the drops rattling on the oiled leather. And then he thought sadly of the forest creatures who had no snug place to shelter from the storm.

The boy liked his Winter home. He liked to lie awake at night, snug in his Winter clothes and fox-fur hood, smothered in a bearskin rug. He listened to the boisterous spirits in the wind who plucked at the roof of the house. He listened to the shrill voices and fretful footsteps of the small creatures who rustled among the thatch. The boy was soothed by the warm bodies and sleeping sounds of his father and mother, sisters and brothers all cosily wedged around him in the Winter house. And then he thought of the forest creatures who slept all Winter long in their own thick fur in beds of leaves and dark lairs.

The boy liked his Winter home

Life was good for the people of the forest. The wildwood gave them all they could need. On hunting days the boy went into the forest with his father and his two big brothers. His father was a mighty hunter. He was as strong as a boar. He was as fearless as the angry aurochs (the fierce wild bull of the forest). He was as patient as the lynx (the cruel spotted cat of the wildwood). He prowled like the silent fox making no sound as he hunted among the trees. And so his name was Hunts-as-the-Forest-Spirit.

The boy's father taught his sons well. He showed them how to make sharp knives and arrowheads from the flints they gathered in a secret place. It was a fearful place of great rocks and caverns where dangerous spirits dwelled. The good father showed his sons how to make traps and set snares for small animals. Sometimes the boy's traps caught a lithe polecat or a marten. These hunting creatures were not good eating, but their fur made snug collars for Winter clothes and mittens for the coldest days. The boy felt sad when he saw a creature caught in his trap. He turned away and could not look when his rough big brother took the warm body from his snare.

The mighty hunter and his boys tracked the wide-eyed deer who hid among the trees or came to browse on green leaves in a forest clearing. The boys learned to follow the dainty footprints of the great red deer and the timid roe. They lay still and made no sound while the gentle creatures strayed close. Then they loosed the wasp-sharp arrows from their bows. But then the soft-hearted boy would turn away. He did not like to watch when his father and his heavy-footed brothers burst from their hiding place. They rushed out with their fierce hunters' cries and their flint-bladed spears. They fell like wolves upon the wounded deer. But deer meat was good eating. And the boy's skilful mother made the doeskin into fine soft shirts and leggings and silent hunter's shoes.

There was boar in the forest—fierce but good eating. The boy's big brothers both wore boar's tusks on strings around their necks. The savage magic charms showed how brave they were. The yellow ivory gave them strength and brought good luck when hunting. The boy liked the dark pork that his mother roasted in the embers of the campfire. But, even as he wiped the grease from his chin or picked the crackling from his teeth, the boy felt sorry for the creature. And, as he curled up to sleep with a full belly, he wondered whether somewhere in the forest there was a den of piglets waiting, fearful and hungry, for a mother who would not return.

One day, when hunting with his father, he found a bear cub alone in the forest. The fat brown baby was caught in a thicket. It was crying for its mother. The boy's father put an arrow to his bow. He crept close. He aimed the flint barb at the creature's throat.

But as the arrow left the bow, the boy sprang forward. He tried to snatch the arrow from the air. It burned through his fingers leaving a stinging scar on his hand. The arrow missed its mark. It shrieked away into the dim distance. It struck a tree and the flint tip shattered.

The boy's father stared at his son aghast. What soft-hearted madness was this! Had some spirit possessed his son? Could this tender-hearted boy be the son of a mighty hunter? The father watched in astonishment as his son spoke in his soft voice to calm the terrified creature. Then he carefully released it from the clutching thorns. The cub made no sound. It stared deep into the boy's eyes. Then it scampered away into the undergrowth and out of sight.

The boy's father stared at his son aghast.

The boy felt a warm joy within his spirit. His father was sad and disappointed.
He was ashamed of his son.

The boy was the youngest of his family. He had three brothers. The oldest,
though, had already gone away. He had found a wife among the tribe that
pitched its shelters by the faraway sea. And now he lived with the hunters of the
shore. The boy's two remaining brothers were almost grown up. They were as
brave as men. They were as tall as their father, though not so strong or knowing
in the ways of the wildwood. But they had many stories to tell of their adventures
in the forest and their fearless hunting. Their deeds gave them their names: so
one was called Angry-Aurochs, after the fierce wild bull of the forest which he
had killed; the other was named Wrestles-the-Wolf.

The boy was young. He had no tales to tell. His father sometimes looked sadly
at his youngest child. He shook his head and wondered how this boy would ever
grow cunning, strong and fierce enough to live the hunter's life. The boy's big
brothers teased him. They called him Small-No-Name.

Sometimes the boy found an excuse to stay in the camp while the men went hunting. He liked to be among the gentle laughing women-folk. He liked the chatter of his clever mother and his busy sisters—some of whom already had babes of their own.

Of course the women and girls did not hunt. How could they? They were not strong and quick like men. A girl could not chase the quick deer with a babe in a sling at her breast. A woman could not follow the boar as it battered through the thickets—not with a clutch of children clinging to the fringes of her coat.

The women's work was to tend the fire that burned all day and night upon a hearth of stones. Their work was to scrape and soften the skins of creatures that the hunters killed. They sewed them into clothes. The women spent long days plaiting baskets from the pliable willow. They made ropes and hunters' nets from twisted grass and nettle stems. They made magic, medicine and babies—and songs at the fireside.

The women gathered the fruits of the forest in due season. With antler picks and digging sticks they dug for roots beneath the frozen floor of the Winter wild-wood. They found birds' eggs in the Spring. They took their baskets and picked raspberries and strawberries in the glades of Summer. The boy went with his sisters when the blackberries gleamed in the thickets. They returned at dusk with birch-bark buckets brimful, their happy faces and scratched hands all stained with rosy berry juice. In Autumn the women took their leather bags and woven baskets to gather the rattling harvest of hazel nuts. And sometimes the boy watched his mother gather the pretty poisonous fruits she used for medicine and magic.

But, as the boy grew older, the women became uneasy. It was not right that a boy who was nearly a man should know their secrets. His father, meanwhile, was troubled that his son had not yet become a cunning hunter, able to live the forest life. And all the boy's big brothers and sisters were dismayed that he had not yet earned himself a name.

One day, the boy's father spoke seriously to his son. "The time has come," he said, "for you to find a name and become a man. And so tomorrow when the moon is full, you will go alone into the forest. You will take no food. You will stay two days and one night in the wildwood. When you return you will tell the tale of your adventure at the fireside. Then you will be a man and we shall know your name."

Early next morning the boy's mother kissed him. His father gave him a flint-bladed spear, a stiff new bow and a sheaf of flint-tipped arrows. Then, all alone, the boy walked into the forest.

He set some traps and snares. He hoped that he would catch something for his supper. Then he went a-hunting. He hoped he would make a great kill. Then his father would be proud and he would have a name. All day he hunted. He saw the tracks of a deer. But he did not see the deer who made the tracks. He saw a tuft of badger fur on a thorn. But he did not see the badger. He hunted until the woodland grew dim. He hunted until he was tired and hungry. But the forest creatures all hid from the hunting boy.

The boy returned to his traps. A slim squirrel struggled, caught by the leg in a snare. Here, at least, was a supper. The boy drew the small axe with its head of chipped flint from his belt.

"Oh do not hurt me, sir!"

The boy started with surprise.

"Oh do not hurt me, sir!" the squirrel said again in a shrill squirrel voice.

"But I must kill you," said the boy. "I must kill you for my supper."

"Oh spare me, sir. Spare me, mighty hunter," begged the squirrel. "I have kits in my drey up in the treetop. They too want their supper. If I do not bring it they will starve and die."

"I must kill you so that I can have a name and become a man," said the boy.

"But you have a name already. It is known to all the forest, though it is unknown to you. Let me live and I will help you find your name."

The squirrel's plea touched the boy's heart. He tucked the axe back into his belt. Then gently he untangled the squirrel from the snare. "Go little friend," he said when it was free. "Go to your kits. I shall become a man another day."

And the squirrel scuttled up the trunk of the nearest tree and bounded away among the branches.

The boy sighed. It was dark now. He had nothing to eat and now must stay out in the wildwood all night. He lay down at the foot of a tree and curled up to sleep.

Next morning he was wakened by the singing of the birds. There was dew in his hair but his clothes were dry, protected from the damp by a covering of leaves. The boy's tummy rumbled hungrily. He had caught nothing and so there was nothing for breakfast. He sat up, shaking the sleep from his brain and the leaves from his clothes. But what was this? A hundred pale hazel nuts, all neatly shelled, were heaped at the foot of the tree. This was a mystery! But the boy was too hungry to think for long about this strange gift of the forest. He munched on the nuts until his stomach was full. Then he made his way back home.

It was evening when the boy arrived at the skin tent beside the whitestone in the heart of the forest. He sat down to eat with his mother and father, his sisters and brothers. When the meal was finished, the whole family listened while the boy told the tale of his hunting. He told of the deer and the badger that he had not seen. He told of the squirrel he had released from the snare. But he did not tell what the squirrel had said. And he did not tell of the mysterious hazel nuts.

Then the boy's mother looked sadly at her son. His sisters were ashamed of their little brother. His father looked disappointed. His big brothers laughed and called him Scared-of-the-Squirrel.

The boy was angry. "That is not my name," he said.

When next the moon was full, the boy's father again spoke seriously to his son. "The time has come," he said, "for you to find a name and become a man. You will go into the forest. You will take no food. You will spend two days and one night in the wildwood. When you return you will tell the tale of your adventure at the fireside. Then you will be a man and we shall know your name."

Next morning the boy's mother kissed him. His father gave him a flint-bladed spear, a stiff new bow and a sheaf of flint-tipped arrows. Then, all alone, the boy walked into the forest.

He set some traps and snares by the waterside. Then he went a-hunting. All day he hunted. He saw the pads of the wolf-pack. But he did not see a wolf. He saw the place where the spotted lynx (the cruel hunting cat of the forest) had made his mark. But he did not see the lynx. In the evening he returned to his traps. A fat beaver struggled in a cunning trap of wood and wicker at the waterside. The boy drew the small axe with its head of chipped flint from his belt.

"Oh do not hurt me, sir!"

The boy started with surprise.

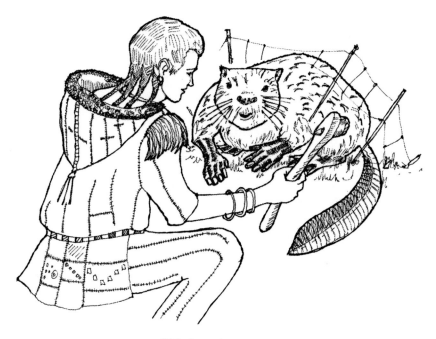

"Oh do not hurt me, sir!"

"Oh do not hurt me, sir!" the beaver said again in a gruff beaver voice.

"But I must kill you," said the boy. "I must kill you for my supper."

"Oh spare me, sir. Spare me, mighty hunter," pleaded the beaver. "I have a wife and cubs in my lodge of sticks in the lake. They too want their supper. If I do not bring it to them they will starve and die."

"I must kill you so that I can have a name and become a man," said the boy.

"But you have a name already. It is known to all the forest, though it is unknown to you. Let me live and I will help you find your name."

The beaver's plea touched the boy's heart. He tucked the axe back into his belt. Then he released the beaver from the trap. "Go good father," he said. "Go to your family. I shall become a man another day."

The boy sighed. It was dark now. He had nothing to eat and now must stay out in the wildwood all night. He lay down at the waterside and curled up to sleep.

Next morning he was wakened by the splash of a fish in the water. There was dew in his hair but his clothes were dry, protected from the damp by a covering of leaves. The boy's tummy rumbled hungrily. But he had caught nothing so there was nothing for breakfast. He sat up, shaking the sleep from his brain and the leaves from his clothes. He shivered. It was a cold morning and the mist from the water made everything chill and damp. But what was this? A hundred pale hazel nuts, all neatly shelled, were heaped on the grass. And a pile of dry sticks, just right for a fire, lay by his sleeping place. This was a mystery! But the boy was too chilled and hungry to think for long about these gifts from the forest. He quickly lit a fire. And when the dry sticks were crackling, he warmed his hands and hungrily munched the nuts until his stomach was full. Then he made his way back home

It was evening when the boy arrived at the skin tent beside the whitestone in the heart of the forest. He sat down to eat with his father and mother, his sisters and brothers. When the meal was finished, the whole family listened while the boy told the tale of his hunting. He told of the wolf and the lynx he had not seen. He told of the beaver he had released from the trap. But he did not tell of the hazel nuts or the sticks for his fire.

Then the boy's mother looked sadly at her son. His sisters were ashamed of their little brother. His father looked disappointed. His brothers laughed loudly and called him Afraid-of-the-Beaver.

The boy was angry. "That is not my name," he said.

When next the moon was full, the boy's father again spoke seriously to his son. "The time has come," he said, "for you to find a name and become a man. You will go into the forest. You will take no food. You will stay two days and one night in the wildwood. When you return you will tell the tale of your adventure at the fireside. Then you will be a man and we shall know your name."

Next morning the boy's mother kissed him. His father gave him a flint-bladed spear, a stiff new bow and a sheaf of flint-tipped arrows. Then, all alone, the boy walked into the forest.

He set some traps and snares. Then he went a-hunting. He saw the mud-puddle where the boar had rolled. But he did not see the boar. He saw a feather from the buzzard's wing. But he did not see or hear the soaring bird. In the evening he returned to his traps. As he came near the place he heard a frightened shriek. He crept close with a hunter's silent footsteps. A fox had found his traps. It was a sly vixen. She had taken a fat water vole from the trap. She had killed the vole. She had eaten it. The end of its tail hung from the corner of the vixen's mouth. The boy crept close. He struck the vixen with the shaft of his spear. The creature fell, stunned. The boy drew the small axe with its head of chipped flint from his belt. He raised the axe. As he did so the vixen opened her yellow eyes.

"Oh do not hurt me, sir!"

The boy started with surprise.

"Oh do not hurt me, sir," barked the vixen again in a fierce and foxy voice.

"But I must kill you, because you have eaten my supper," said the boy.

"But I have a litter of cubs waiting for me in my earth," pleaded the creature. "They too want their supper. If I do not return they will starve and die."

"I must kill you so that I may have a name and become a man," said the boy.

"But you have a proper name already. It is known to all the forest, though it is unknown to you. Let me live and I will help you find your name."

The vixen's plea touched the boy's heart. He tucked the axe back into his belt. Then he helped the vixen to her feet. "Go, good mother," he said. "Go to your cubs. I shall become a man another day."

The boy sighed. It was dark now. He had nothing to eat and now must stay out in the wildwood all night. He lay down on the ground and curled up to sleep.

Next morning he was wakened by the dawn light flooding through the trees. There was dew in his hair but his clothes were dry, protected from the damp by a covering of leaves. His tummy rumbled hungrily. But he had caught nothing so there was nothing for breakfast. He sat up, shaking the sleep from his brain and the leaves from his clothes. But what was this? A hundred pale hazel nuts, all neatly shelled, were piled on the grass. A heap of dry sticks, just right for a fire, lay by his sleeping place. And, stretched out by the sticks, was a fat brown hare— freshly killed and good eating. This was a mystery! But the boy was too cold and hungry to think for long about these gifts from the forest. He quickly kindled a fire. He munched on the hazel nuts while he roasted the hare. Then, with a full stomach, he made his way home.

... a fat brown hare—freshly killed and good eating

It was evening when the boy arrived at the skin tent beside the whitestone in the heart of the forest. He sat down to eat with his father and mother, sisters and brothers. When the meal was finished, the whole family listened to the tale of the boy's hunting. He told of the boar and the buzzard that he had not seen. He told of the vixen he had spared. But he did not tell of the hazel nuts, nor of the sticks for his fire or the fat brown hare.

Then the boy's mother looked sadly at her son. His sisters were ashamed of their little brother. His father looked disappointed. His big brothers laughed loudly and called him Fooled-by-the-Fox.

The boy was angry. "That is not my name," he said.

When next the moon was full, the boy's father again spoke seriously to his son. "The time has come," he said, "for you to find your name and become a man. You will go into the forest. You will take no food. You will stay two days and one night in the wildwood. When you return you will tell the tale of your adventure at the fireside. Then you will be a man and we shall know your name."

Next morning the boy's mother kissed him. His father gave him a flint-bladed spear, a stiff new bow and a sheaf of flint-tipped arrows. Then, all alone, the boy walked into the forest.

He set some traps and snares. Then he went a-hunting. All day he hunted, but he saw no sign of any creature. All he heard was the singing of the birds. Their song rang all around his head. In the evening he returned to his traps. All were empty. And now it began to rain. The boy searched for a place to sleep and found at last a deep dry cave. He crept inside. He sighed. He had nothing to eat. He lay down and curled up to sleep.

Next morning he was wakened by a distant sound of human voices. There was dew in his hair but his clothes were dry, protected from the damp by a covering of leaves. His tummy rumbled hungrily. But he had caught nothing so there was nothing for breakfast. He sat up, shaking the sleep from his brain and the leaves from his clothes. He looked around him. By his side were a hundred pale hazel nuts, neatly shelled, and a pile of sticks, just right for a fire, and a fat brown hare, freshly killed and good eating. And suddenly there was his father and mother, his sisters and brothers too. They were all smiling and singing a song of joy.

Mother and sisters kissed the boy. Father and brothers clapped him on the back. Then, still singing with delight, they carried the bewildered boy home. They carried him back to their camp beside the whitestone in the heart of the forest. When they reached the skin tent they sat down to eat. They feasted on forest pork with hazel nuts and roast hare. When the meal was finished, the boy's father said, "Now I shall tell the story of our boy's great hunting. I shall tell the tale of how this boy became a man and how he found his name."

The boy was astonished. He had hunted nothing. He had done nothing that could make him a man or let him know his name.

"We watched the boy," his father began, "as he walked in the forest. We followed with quiet footsteps while he hunted. We heard the birds call warnings to the forest creatures, who hid because there was a mighty man in their wildwood. No creature dared come near his traps and snares. We saw the boy curl up to sleep in the dark cave. It was cold. He shivered in his sleep. And then the great bear came. She lay beside the boy to keep him warm—as though he were her own dear cub. She kept him warm and safe all night, and then she went away. We watched while woodland birds dropped leaves on the boy to keep him from the dews. We saw a hundred squirrels come. Each brought one pale hazel nut, neatly shelled. We saw the beaver come. He came with his wife and his cubs. They brought dry sticks, just right for a fire. We saw a red vixen come. She brought a fat brown hare, newly killed and good eating. We saw all the forest caring for the boy because his heart was kind."

And then the great bear came.

The boy looked at his brothers. They did not laugh at him. They beamed with pride because their brother was a man and he had found his name.

"Our boy is now a mighty man," his father continued. "He is mightier than all the cunning hunters of the forest—because he speaks the language of the wild-wood, because he cares for all its creatures. His name is known to all the forest—to the birds and to the squirrel, to the beaver and the vixen and the bear—though it was not known to us till now. This boy, who is the youngest, is the best of all my sons. And his name is He-Whom-All-the-Forest-Loves."

CHAPTER 3

▼

KINDNESS AND STRANGERS

The Girl Lightfoot lived the best life of all in the long long long-ago time. She belonged to the people of the cliff-foot. And she was happy to share with her mother and father, her cousins and aunts and her friends, the gentle world of the seashore.

She thought there was no happier sound than the clatter and hiss of the waves breaking on the beach. She thought there was no more comforting voice than the cry of the grey gull that skimmed on stiff wings along the cliff face. She thought there was no better place than the big seashore camp at the foot of the cliff.

Her own shelter was the finest of all the seashore houses. Her father had built it against the cliff where overhanging rocks gave shelter from the weather. The house was made of driftwood that the sea brought to the shore, and sturdy branches cut with a flint axe in the forest that came right to the cliff-edge. The girl's mother stretched oiled skins across the roof. And The Girl Lightfoot gathered sharp grasses from the sand dunes. She helped to thatch the house and make it snug and dry and dark.

The people of the cliff-foot.

The people of the cliff-foot were a contented clan. They made their shelters and lived together without fighting or harsh words, because the sea was good to them. Under a sky of skirling gulls, in the shadow of the cliff, they found all that they could need.

They did not live here all the time. For a season the clan left the seashore. The women packed up the skin shelters in tight-rolled bundles. The children shouldered baskets containing the family's possessions. The men too carried heavy loads—as well as their spears and bows. Then the families bade farewell to one another. They promised to meet again soon at the cliff-foot campsite. Each family went its own way, melting away into the forest: each to make its own camp; each to hunt the wild creatures and gather the forest fruits for a long season.

The Girl Lightfoot liked this quiet time. She drew close to her mother who taught her many secrets. She liked the food her father hunted. She liked the softness of the warm furs—fox, otter, marten and beaver—that her father trapped and that she stitched into warm Winter clothes. She liked the stillness of the green places among the trees and the shy sounds of the woodland creatures. But soon she yearned for the broad skies and the loud birds and the jolly companionship of the big camp on the seashore. And she was glad when her father said it was time to return.

The generous seashore gave the people of the cliff-foot everything they could need. The Girl Lightfoot leaped and scrambled among the slippery rocks. She splashed barefoot among the rock pools. With quick fingers she gathered the cockles and coiled whelks into her basket. She tempted the scuttling crabs from beneath the rocks, then snatched them up and clattered them in with the shells. Her anxious mother told her not to go beyond the near headland. But The Girl Lightfoot was unafraid. She went far beyond the near headland to where the largest limpets and the blackest mussels grew upon the rocks. When she returned her mother scolded her for going so far. And then her mother clapped her hands with delight when she saw her daughter's basket filled with the largest limpets and the blackest plumpest mussels.

The Girl Lightfoot helped her mother prepare and cook the seafood feast. She sat beside her father at the campfire while he ate his evening meal and told her of his day's hunting. After they had eaten, she tipped the broken shells onto the midden-heap that grew, season by season under a swirl of scavenging gulls, at the far end of the beach.

In the Spring, The Girl Lightfoot scrambled on the tall cliffs. Her anxious mother told her not to climb too high. But she climbed to the giddying ledges where the auks and grey gulls nested. She gathered the pale and blue and brown-specked eggs from beneath the birds who gaped and shrieked and flapped and spat. But they did not frighten the nimble thief. A moon passed and she climbed the cliffs again. She scurried, quick as a lizard, along the ledges to pluck fluffy fledglings from the nests while their mothers were at sea.

She returned to her mother who scolded her for being so daring. She returned to her mother who was delighted with the fine fat birds she had caught. Then the feathers flew as The Girl Lightfoot helped to pluck the warm catch. They saved the downy feathers to stuff into thick padded Winter coats. They roasted the birds on their campfire for a suppertime feast.

The girl's father went fishing with the other menfolk. He owned a fine log boat. The Girl Lightfoot remembered the day when she went with her father into the forest. He took a big flint axe to cut the trunk of a great fallen tree. She had watched the men drag it back to the beach. Then, for a long season, her father had worked with fire and a flint axe to hollow out the boat. He fitted an outrigger so that the narrow craft would not overturn when the sea was rough. He carved a fine paddle, decorated it with patterned bands. And the wiseman of the cliff-foot folk begged a blessing on the boat from all the quarrelsome, contrary spirits of the sea and the wind.

He owned a fine log boat.

The men went in log boats and skittish skin canoes to fish with bone hooks for the gaping cod. Sometimes they caught a great grey shark. Sometimes they caught nothing. Sometimes they drove a small whale or dolphin into the shallows where they killed it with their spears. Sometimes the shrieking gulls and diving gannets told them that a shoal of herring had come into the bay. Then they hurried out with nets in their boats. Everyone became excited because there would be a feast of rich fish and much left over, which the women smoked and dried to feed their families when the seas were rough and the boats could not go out.

In the Autumn-time, as the days shortened, the camp became busy and excited. The women and girls stitched warm fur clothing for the Winter. They went in small groups into the forest. They stayed for several days gathering fruits and fungi. They returned with the smell of campfire smoke in their hair and baskets on their backs filled with glossy hazel nuts.

In the Autumn-time the seals came. They lay lumpishly on the beach nursing their wide-eyed pups. Big bull seals bullied and blustered and bothered the gentle mothers. The men of the cliff-foot made their preparations. The Girl Lightfoot begged and begged to be allowed to watch the hunt. She begged her mother. She begged her father. She begged them both at dawn and dusk. At last her father agreed that his little girl might come with him on the seal hunt.

And so The Girl Lightfoot sat proudly in the stern of the bobbing log boat, a small paddle in her hand. Her father steadied the boat with his broad carved paddle. A harpoon with a barbed bone point lay ready to hand. The plaited line lay coiled in the bottom of the boat. Father and daughter watched the shore. Two groups of hunters with spears and bows crept, snakelike, on their bellies across the sands. The lazy seals dozed in the sunshine. They did not see the men.

Then, too late, they saw the men. The hunters rushed forward. The seals heard the shriek of arrows. Too late. The arrows stung into their fat flanks. Too late. The men fell upon their prey. Flint-bladed spears found their mark and three mother seals lay dead. Three pups blinked with dazed orphan eyes at the men who stood over them. The rest of the seals fled fatly over the shingle and butted into the waves. Now the hunt was in the sea.

The Girl Lightfoot and her father waited. The harpoon was in her father's fist. The long shaft lay on his shoulder. Suddenly a big-eyed face rose to take a breath. A scar-faced bull seal stared for a moment at the man and the girl. Then, as the big bull dived, the strong man's arm plunged the harpoon into the sleek body. The barbed bone point seared through the skin and blubber. It jagged into the muscle below. The coiled line hissed as the bull seal vanished beneath the boat. But then the line snagged. With a jolt the boat was dragged through the waves. The canoe raced across the wave-tops towards to open sea beyond the bay. The girl's father touched the coil to free the line, but it tangled around his wrist. It jerked tight. The girl shrieked as her father was pitched from the boat into the water. The flight of the wounded bull seal dragged him under. But, quick as thought, the hunter reached a flint blade from his pocket. He cut the line and bobbed to the surface.

He came into the air a long way from the boat. He raised a hand to show he was unhurt. His daughter returned his wave. She dug deep with her paddle to turn the boat towards her father. But the boat would not turn. The strong current that flowed across the mouth of the bay took the log boat in its grip. The boat sped seaward despite the girl's fierce panic of paddling. Her father was a strong swimmer. But he could not outswim the current that carried his boat and his daughter away. Treading water, the hunter watched, hopeless. Then he turned his back. He swam towards the shore—to the small skin boats that were coming to his rescue.

A cool mist drew across the sea. And suddenly The Girl Lightfoot did not know which way the beach lay. She stopped paddling. She shouted into the clammy fog. No voice replied. The boat bobbed cheerfully. But the lost girl did not feel at all cheerful.

For a long time the girl shouted into the mist. For a long time no voice—not even a mewing gull—replied. Then the girl knew she had drifted far from the shore. She paddled gently though she did not know which way she should go. Now and then the pointed prow of the boat nosed playfully into the front of a wave. It dipped, like a bird drinking, and a splash of water gurgled into the boat. Then the girl stopped paddling. She took the carved wooden cup that was tied with a string to the side of the boat and bailed the water back into the sea. But, however much she bailed, still the water sloshed around her feet.

... a splash of water gurgled into the boat.

Now and then the boat rolled. Then the outrigger lifted from the water. It slapped happily back onto the next wave with a jolly splash. But The Girl Lightfoot did not feel at all jolly. She knew she was in grave danger. Only the bravest (or the most foolish) of her people went out among the mischievous spirits of the sea mist. Nobody ever went out of sight of land. The Girl Lightfoot did not feel at all brave.

She tried to steer the boat so that the waves came from behind. Surely the next wave would carry her to the shore. Or perhaps the next wave—or the next, or the next—would sweep her onto her own safe beach. And there would be her father looking sad and her mother looking stern—and both full of joy that she was safe.

A wind sprang up. The girl Lightfoot sniffed the rising breeze. It carried no familiar smells: no hint of campfire smoke, no cooking aromas, not even the comforting stink of the cliff-foot midden.

The girl Lightfoot peered into the mist. She expected at any moment to see the ragged white breaking waves at the edge of the sea. She strained her eyes for the loom of the cliffs against the sky. But there was only the chilly grey mist and the salt smell of the sea.

It was cold. Her hair dripped icy water down her bare back. The wind whipped flurries of spray from the wave-tops and flung them like stinging handfuls of salt against her bare arms. The sea became more boisterous. Wicked spirits danced in the wave-crests. Water splashed into the boat faster than the girl could bail. Now it covered her feet. The cold gripped her ankles.

Now the girl knew that she would never see her mother and father again. Soon she would die of cold and drowning. A terrible shivering ran through her small body. Soon she would hear the Great Spirit as he came to take her from the world. She wondered how he would come. Would he come on broad white wings like a swan? Or would he stride across the face of the ocean?

Yes! She could hear him. She stopped bailing. It was no use. Better to be still and wait. It would not be long now. She began to sing. Her thin voice sang through chattering teeth. She sang in high notes the song her people made to welcome the Great Spirit. She had heard the song when elders closed their eyes and when babes were too frail for the world. She had heard it sung for hunters who—more brave than cunning—fell prey to the bristling boar and angry aurochs (the fierce wild bull of the forest).

The Girl Lightfoot heard the Spirit quite clearly now. His footstep was a dull and rhythmic *thud-and-splash, thud-and-splash* on the water.

Thud-and-splash, thud-and-splash.

The Great Spirit was coming for her.

Thud-and-splash, thud-and-splash.

The girl's shivering stopped. A strange sleepiness came over her. A comfortable dreaminess warmed her from within.

Thud-and splash, thud-and-splash.

Then suddenly, like a hunter bursting from a thicket, the prow of a great dark boat broke from the mist. The girl stopped singing. This was unexpected. She had not thought the Great Spirit would come in a boat. The prow of the boat—a big wood-framed skin boat—butted the waves aside.

… the prow of a great dark boat broke from the mist.

Thud-and-splash, thud-and-splash.

Big paddles dug into the sea. They churned the water aside.

Thud-and-splash, thud-and-splash.

The boat tore a foaming furrow through the water.

And now a second boat appeared; and a third; and another and another. Now there was a shout. A strange spirit voice cried out. A chorus of spirit voices replied from within the mist. The big boats bore down on the little girl as her water-logged canoe rolled sluggishly among the waves.

In a confusion of gruff shouts and shrill cries The Girl Lightfoot felt herself lifted. She was dragged, sprawlingly, from the log boat. Bewildered and numbed by cold, she wondered that the Great Spirit should have such rough clumsy hands. But now, in a flurry of strange voices, she was wrapped in a scratchy cloak that smelled like no animal she had ever known. And she was cradled in hot round arms, smothered in the warm smell of women. Like a newborn babe she nuzzled into the cosiness. She closed her eyes and let the Great Spirit take her. She drifted away to the sound of his footsteps on the water.

Thud-and-splash, thud-and-splash, thud-and-splash.

It was long before the girl woke. Was she a spirit? She did not feel like a spirit. Her mouth was dry and full of salt. The cloak around her shoulders chafed her skin. She shivered and buried her face in the warmth that surrounded her. A gentle hand stroked her hair.

The girl opened her eyes. She started in fear and surprise. She stared into a face—a stranger's face—a strange face. It was not the face of her own people. The lips of the strange face moved. They made sounds she had never heard before. They spoke no words she could understand. The girl struggled, but the arms that held her were strong. The lips murmured sounds that might have been soft and comforting. But still there were no human words.

The girl looked around. She was tightly wrapped in strange furs and skins, tightly clasped in the arms of a strange strong woman. They were huddled in the stern of the boat. Four burly men hunched their shoulders and dug deep with their paddles. The heavy boat moved grudgingly. The craft was crammed with bags and bundles, baskets and strange containers that might have been made of stone—but were not made of stone. There were animals too. Big thick-furred beasts with yellow eyes and coiling horns were trussed up in the bottom of the boat. Their panting bodies and bleating breath warmed the girl's feet.

The girl at last found her voice. "Oh do not take me yet, Great Spirit. I am only small. Do not kill me, spirit people!" she cried.

The stranger woman smiled. She said a word. She lifted a gritty stone cup to the girl's lips. The Girl Lightfoot was as thirsty as a babe at the breast. She swallowed the strange rich drink. It was thick and slick. It smelled of grass. The woman dipped a morsel into the drink and offered it to the girl's lips. Suspiciously The Girl Lightfoot tasted the strange spirit food. It melted on her tongue. It was not meat. It was not hazel nuts. It was not fruit or fungi. She ate hungrily. The woman spoke again. The Girl Lightfoot understood not a word. But she understood kindness in the voice. And she smiled.

"Thank you for saving me," murmured The Girl Lightfoot. And the stranger woman smiled too.

Now the men began to shout. The women called from one boat to another. A moment later the boats broke from the mist into bright sunshine. The stroke of the paddles quickened. Another moment and the bottom of the boat grated on a shingle beach. The men leaped into the breaking waves. They moved awkwardly, their limbs stiff with cold and long sitting. But they moved in a flurry of excited activity. They dragged the boats onto the beach. They danced and capered. They shouted with joy.

The women rose from their seats. They lifted their skirts and stepped over the high sides of the boats. A group of older women squatted on the sand. They began a strange chant. They poured some of the white drink onto the ground. Then they smashed the bowl.

The stranger woman lifted The Girl Lightfoot and carried her up the beach. The girl stood, afraid and fascinated, watching as the strange folk began to unload their boats. With sharp flint knives they cut the cords that bound the feet of their animals. They tethered the thick-fleeced skittishly complaining creatures among some rocks where there was grass for them to eat. Boys and girls gathered driftwood and made a fire. The stranger folk sat down together. They shared their strange food. A stranger girl came from the tethered animals. She carried a bowl of the white drink. The people laughed and sang. They helped one another. They dressed each other's hair in plaits and braids with tinkling beads, feathers and coloured tassels. A little boy took The Girl Lightfoot by the hand. He led her to the fireside to join the feast.

A shout broke through the strangers' happy chatter. The men leaped to their feet. They stood in front of their women. Each held a long-handled axe with a head of glossy black stone. The axes gleamed. The Girl Lightfoot had never seen such weapons before. Some of the men also held long flint-bladed spears. Some boys ran to the boats. They pulled tall bows from among the bundles. They fumbled to find the bowstrings and bring them with quivers of arrows to the men. The girl saw the arrowheads were shaped like the leaf of a beechtree—not like the tiny sharp flint slivers that made the barbed points of her own people's arrows.

The shriek of an arrow sliced through the breathless hush that had fallen over the strangers. A warning arrow thudded into a tuffock of thrift. A group of cliff-foot men was running towards the strangers. Each man carried a bow with an arrow nocked to the string. The running men halted. They took aim with their bows.

"No!"

The Girl Lightfoot rushed forward. She spread her arms wide as if to protect the strangers with her little body. The cliff-foot men hesitated. They lowered their bows. A man stepped forward. He cast away his bow and ran towards the strangers. And a moment later The Girl Lightfoot was swept from her feet and whirled in the strong arms of her joyful father.

The stranger women smiled a deep and knowing smile. Their men remained on guard.

"Father!" the girl stammered. "You must not hurt these people. They saved me from the waves. They gave me life when the Great Spirit came to take me. Though they are strangers, they are friends."

The stranger men lowered their spears. A round strong woman stepped up and spoke her strange words to the girl's father. The wiseman of the cliff-foot folk came forward. But he was disconcerted. Among his people only men spoke words of importance. But among these strangers it was the women who spoke and the men who quietly obeyed.

The wiseman and the stranger woman spoke in words that neither understood. They spoke in signs. They spoke in tones of friendship. The woman offered a gift. It was a pot containing bright white salt. The cliff-foot wiseman looked at the gift. He wondered why folk should have such a bulky container. It was far too heavy to carry when wandering between camps. But he bowed and thanked her in a stately tone.

And then the two peoples parted. The Girl Lightfoot wished she had some words or a gift to give the strangers. But she had no words and nothing to give.

*   *   *   *

Reunited with her parents, The Girl Lightfoot told the tale of her adventure. It was a long story—the best kind for an Autumn fireside. She showed the strange cloak which the stranger woman had cast around her shoulders. The women fingered it delightedly; and long into the night they discussed how it was made and from what strange creature it came.

But the wiseman was not pleased. He cast away his bowl of salt. It shattered into a dozen pieces. He said that evil spirits travelled in the strangers' boats. He prophesied that the cliff-foot people would wither and die like flowers when the frost comes. Most, though, took no notice. They said that their elder was old and foolish. They admired the strangers. They envied their big boats and black axes— and their fancy clothes.

But the girl's father knew the elder was wise. Her mother was uneasy, like a forest deer when wolves are nearby. And before a quarter moon had passed, The Girl Lightfoot and her father and mother packed their skin tent and their baskets and melted away into the forest.

But no evil came. The Winter was mild. Spring came early. The Summer was hot. And the next Autumn was more fruitful than any the girl's mother could remember. The hunting was good. Deer and boar came to her father's ambush. Small game came to his traps. It was the best year he had known. They shifted camp several times, and each new place brought better hunting and finer forest fruits. The Girl Lightfoot declared that the strangers had brought good spirits from beyond the sea. And she and her father and mother lived for two full years in the forest which was more generous even than the fruitful seaside.

At last, though, they grew homesick for the sound of the sea. They travelled back to the familiar seaside place beneath the gull-wheeling skies. But when they arrived, there was no busy campsite at the cliff-foot. Their house had tumbled down. The midden was covered with grass. Only two shelters stood in the shadow of the rearing cliff. In one the people were sick. In the other the old wiseman sat gloomily staring into the embers of a dying fire.

"Where are our people?" the girl's father cried in alarm. "Where is the laughter of our great family of the seashore?"

The old man looked up. There were tears in his eyes.

"Oh, you were wise to go to the forest. But most were not so wise. They would not hear the words and warnings that the spirits brought to my lips. And now they are all gone."

"Gone? Gone where?" cried the girl's father.

"Gone to the Great Spirit," the old man replied. "Gone forever from the world."

Gradually the old man told what had happened. He told how the strangers had come with gifts of pots and flint to exchange for fish, furs and seal meat. And when they departed they left behind strange sicknesses that carried off both young and old. He told how some of the young men had gone to the strangers' camp hoping to find wives. But the fierce women had bewitched them so they wasted away and died. He told how some young men had gone hunting in the wildwood. They had killed one of the strangers' animals as it browsed in the forest. Then the stranger men had lain in wait and in revenge they had killed the young men with their black stone axes. And now scarcely any of the cliff-foot folk remained.

"Go back," the wiseman urged. "Flee from the strangers' evil. Go back to the forest."

With heavy hearts, The Girl Lightfoot and her father and mother shouldered their loads. They saw that the cliff-foot had become a place of evil spirits. They would never live there again. They turned their faces towards the forest. They thought they would walk far away—deep into the wildwood—beyond the reach of the strangers' evil.

They walked for three days. All that time there was a smell of smoke in the air, yet they found no hunters' campsites. On the fourth day they came into a place where all the trees were sick. The place was filled with the strangers' shaggy creatures. They lowered their coiling horns and stared at The Girl Lightfoot with wicked yellow eyes. Then they went on with their feeding. Their sharp teeth cropped the grass to the root and peeled the bark from the forest trees. Here and there a clearing had been made. A fierce spirit had used a great axe to fell the trees. And between the ragged stumps the earth was burned black and slashed with savage scars. The girl shuddered. Surely evil spirits were at work.

On the fifth day, the smell of smoke grew stronger. The girl and her family broke from the trees into a large clearing. Tall wooden houses stood where the forest trees should have grown. In the centre of the clearing a round and mothering whitestone boulder swelled from the earth. And all around, the soil where the wildwood rooted was ripped open. At the margins men were at work. They chopped at the great trees with shiny black stone axes. They piled up heaps of stones. Women scattered seeds into the wounded earth. And all the air was filled with the swirl of smoke from brushwood fires. The Girl Lightfoot recoiled in horror. Her father stared, aghast. Her mother turned away, unable to bear the sight.

"The poor trees!" cried The Girl Lightfoot. "The strangers are burning the forest!"

"The strangers are burning the forest!"

CHAPTER 4

▼

THE GIRL WHO MADE
A FRIEND

When she was very young in the long long-ago time, someone asked the little girl, "How old are you?"

Quick as blinking she replied, "I am five Summers old." Then, after a thought as quick as a bee's wingbeat, she added, "... but nearly six."

The simple-serious words stuck in the minds of those who heard. And everyone began to call the girl Five-Summers-Nearly-Six.

At first the little girl grew angry when people called her Five-Summers-Nearly-Six. "That's *not* my name," she said crossly. "I am First-Daughter-of-the-Small-House. *That's* my name."

But the people of the Small Settlement still called her Five-Summers-Nearly-Six. They called her Five-Summers for short. Slowly, the girl became used to her name. And, because nobody used it unkindly, she came at last to like her name. Now, though she was seven Summers old (and nearly eight), she would not change it for all the world.

Five-Summers-Nearly-Six felt special. Nobody else had such a splendid name. She liked to be special. She was special in other ways too. She was special because she was the only child in her mother's small house. She was the only child in a house of grown-ups. And so her soft clever mother and her strong silent father—and especially her grandmother who was wise and full of magic (who saw many things of which she never spoke)—all treated their girl as a special gift. In fact, they spoiled her.

Sometimes, though, Five-Summers did not like to be so special. She looked at the three other big houses of the Small Settlement. Each tall wooden house was filled with capering children, chatter and laughter. Little Five-Summers envied the noisy families in the big houses because her own home was always hushed and serious. Without the happy sound of children's games, the dim corners of her own small house seemed mysterious with voiceless secret things.

Each tall wooden house was filled with capering children.

Five-Summers-Nearly-Six was lonely sometimes—and more thoughtful than a little girl should be. But she was not unhappy. How could she be unhappy? Nobody in the Small Settlement was unhappy. The Sun shone every day to ripen the corn. The rain came softly when the ground was dry and the corn was thirsty. Cattle and sheep grew fat on the grassland beyond the cornfields. And so did the goats that cropped the higher slopes, or wandered at the woodland edge to nip sweet buds and green bark from the young trees.

There could be no unhappiness in the Small Settlement. The people were blessed by all the spirits of earth and air and water. They were blessed by the Sun and the salt-bright Moon. They were blessed by the life that came from the round and milk-white Mothering-Stone who stood at the centre of the fertile fields.

Five-Summers-Nearly-Six learned all the things a girl should know. Her father taught her how to make a sharp flint knife; how to set a snare and skin a hare. And sometimes the girl helped her father herding cattle on the hill.

The clever mother of the small house showed her daughter how to milk the cows and goats and sheep. And Five-Summers helped to make soft cheese and butter from the rich cream. The mother of the small house helped her girl to shape round-bottomed pots from stiff orange clay. She taught her daughter to comb the wool from the complaining sheep, and to spin it into yarn. She built a small loom on which young Five-Summers learned to weave a narrow length of plain soft woollen cloth. The girl could sew a fine seam with her nimble fingers. She learned to grind the corn into flour on the rough rubbing-stone by the fire. She could cook and wash, plait a straw rope and weave a willow basket.

But it was the magical grandmother of the small house (who saw many things of which she never spoke) who taught Five-Summers the most important things. The wise old woman taught her granddaughter the names of all the stars. She taught her to read the skies: to know the time of day and to foretell the weather. She showed her the places where the Sun—at rising and setting—touched the far horizon through the seasons of the year. She explained the mysteries of the strangely-changing Moon who ruled the lives of women. She showed her the medicine of herbs. She whispered secrets in her ear—grown-up magic spells and charms for love and healing. She taught her favourite girl mysterious things that only women know—about the sprouting of the corn and the coming of the lambs in Spring.

The old wise-woman took her granddaughter into the round stone house of the Ancestors. The outside walls of the house were built with giant stones—tall pointed father-stones and rounded mother-stones. The roof was a rounded cairn of rubbly rocks scattered with sparkling magic white-stones. Grandmother of the small house led the way along the low passage that led to the chamber where the Ancestors lived their mysterious life. The wise-woman's broad hips brushed the sides of the passage. Five-Summers followed, stooping so she did not bang her head on the low roof.

Girl and grandmother crouched together in the heart of the Ancestors' house. The stone walls and roof-slabs were carved and painted with circles and zigzags and snaking lines that told the history of the Small Settlement. All around—on shelves and benches and heaped on the floor—were the skulls and bones of the Ancestors. These were the bones of all the people who had lived and died in the Small Settlement. There were the yellowing skulls of great-grandparents; the white teeth of grandmothers and grandfathers. There were the brown bones of the first farmers, who had cleared the forest and made the first fields many many years before. There were broad-jawed men, smiling women and delicate-featured children. And a spirit—an Ancestor—lived in the darkness behind each empty stare.

Girl and grandmother crouched together in the heart of the Ancestors' house.

Five-Summers-Nearly-Six shivered. It was chilly in the house of the dead. She shivered even though this was a place of life. Here the Ancestors lived. They lived forever. The spirits of the Ancestors watched over the Small Settlement and its people. Their breath made the green corn sprout. Their breath made the milk come to the cows and goats. Their glance made the little lambs that played on the pasture in the Spring. The Ancestors came into the houses while the people slept. They made the men strong. They made the women wise and skilful. They made babies.

Five-Summers-Nearly-Six wondered why the Ancestors made no babies in her own small house. They made babies aplenty in the big houses of her friends and cousins. The women of the big houses wondered too. They looked sadly at the father of the small house. They felt sorry for him because he had no sons. They looked askance at the mother of the small house because she had only one daughter. They whispered behind her back. But they never said a word out loud, because they were afraid of the grandmother who was wise and full of magic (and because she saw many things of which she never spoke).

The girl of the small house played with the children from the big houses. But when she went home after a day of capering, singing and laughter, her own home seemed strange and silent. She wished she had a sister or a cousin or a special friend in the small house. She wanted to share her bed with another little girl who would fidget and giggle with her in the darkness. She wanted a sister or a special friend to be all hot and comfortable with her beneath the woollen cloaks and fleeces that covered her snug bed on Winter nights.

The girl named Five-Summers went to the Mothering-Stone—all round and pale as a bonny woman among the fields. With a small finger she traced the wishing-patterns of scrolls and circles that were carved on the smooth flanks and cool strong shoulders of the stone. The girl hugged the stone who was a mother to each and all in the Small Settlement.

"Please, please good Mother-of-All," she begged, "send a sister or a special friend to play with me. I would give the thing I love most in all the world to have a friend to live with me in the small house."

The Mothering-Stone made no reply. But a low whispering among the corn seemed to say, "Beware of wishes. They may come true. Beware of promises that must be kept."

The girl named Five-Summers spoke to the Sun at midday. She stared into his fire-bright eye until her head began to swim. She offered a gift of bread, new-baked by the small house fire. She broke the bread. She ate a piece. She offered a piece to the Sun.

"Please great Life-of-All," she begged, "send a sister or a special friend to play with me. I would give the thing I love most in all the world to have a friend to live with me in the small house."

The Sun rolled on across the sky. He made no sound. But a buzzard mewed overhead. It said, "Beware of wishes. They may come true. Beware of promises that must be kept."

The girl named Five-Summers brought a bowl of milk into the fields at night. She drank a little. She offered it to the Moon. She broke the bowl and scattered the pieces on the ground.

"Please, please sweet Wisdom-of-Women," she begged, "send a sister or a special friend to play with me. I would give the thing I love most in all the world to have a friend to live with me in the small house."

The Moon weaved teasingly in and out of the clouds. She said nothing. But an owl called from the woodland edge. It cried, "Beware of wishes. They may come true."

And a fox cried, "Beware of promises that must be kept."

Bread for the Sun, milk for the Moon

Now the Summer days grew long. The nights grew short. The festival of the Ancestors drew near. The grandmother of the small house spoke with the other wise women. They lit a fire near the entrance to the Ancestors' house. They made an offering of meat and milk. They watched the Sun rise. They waited until it set. They declared that the festival would take place when four sunsets had passed.

Four days were filled with joyful activity.

The women and girls cleaned the big stone house of the Ancestors. They scrubbed the lichen from the fat mother-stones. They scraped the moss from the tall father-stones. The young girls scrambled onto the rubbly cairn. They plucked out the weeds and wildflowers. They scoured each of the magic white-stones that covered the cairn.

The women and the girls decorated the great stones. They painted them with patterns in red and white, black and yellow, purple and orange. They painted the stones with circles and spirals, scrolls and zigzags, spots and dots and curving lines. Their paintings told stories of the life of the Small Settlement. They spoke in the language of wishes and dreams.

Five-Summers-Nearly-Six helped her mother. Together they painted a fat mother-stone. They moved on to the slender father-stone that leaned lovingly against it like a new husband. The girl was too small to reach the top of the tall stone. So, while her mother finished the painting, the girl wandered to the shady side of the Ancestor house. She took a little pot of paint with her.

Furtively she looked around. Nobody was watching. Nimbly as the quick red squirrel, the girl clambered onto the rubbly roof of the Ancestor house. She looked round again—excited and a little frightened. She selected a piece of magic white-stone. She took out her pot of paint. She dipped a finger in the orangey-red colour. With quick movements she began to paint the stone. But she did not make a pattern of rings and wavy lines. She broke the great Law of her people.

SHE PAINTED A PICTURE.

She painted a picture of a little girl like herself—all orangey-red, with orangey-red plaits and an orangey-red skirt and orangey-red bangles on her orangey-red arms and ankles.

A thrill of secret fear filled her heart as she turned the stone over. Her picture was hidden now, face down on the cairn. As she hid her picture, Five-Summers-Nearly-Six muttered a magic word. It was a word of power that her grandmother had taught her—a secret word that Grandmother said no girl should use until she was a grown-up and a mother. But little Five-Summers spoke the word. And she chanted in a quiet serious voice, "Great and strong Ancestors, send a sister or a special friend to play with me. I would give the thing I love most in all the world to have a friend to live with me in the small house."

Five-Summers-Nearly-Six slipped lightly down to the ground. She ran to rejoin her mother.

"Where were you, dear?" her mother asked.

"I just went to look at the other women's paintings." Her voice quavered as she told the lie. And, as she spoke, a little cloud appeared in the sky. It drifted across the Sun. The women stopped work. They looked up. It was a bad sign. The cloud moved away. The women breathed a sigh of relief.

The day of the festival arrived. In the grey time before dawn all the people of the Small Settlement gathered at the house of their Ancestors. They came in their best clothes. Pottery beads jingled the hair of the men. Bracelets of shell from the faraway seashore tinkled on the wrists of the women. Everyone wore bands of fur and feather on their arms and ankles, tassels on their plaits and high head-dresses of bright feathers. The grown-ups were proud of the patterns painted on their breasts and backs.

Young Five-Summers was there with her mother and father. Her grandmother had gone at midnight with the other old women to wait for dawn in the darkness where the Ancestors dwelled. Outside, the people waited, breathlessly.

Now the sky grew pale in the far north-east. Suddenly the Sun burned from below the horizon. He clambered from below the world into the brightest and best dawn of all the long year. He blinked a fierce glance at the people of the Small Settlement gathered around the house of their Ancestors. Then he peered a look of light along the dark passage of the Ancestor house. His bright eye blazed into the chamber where the wise women waited with the skulls and the old brown bones. Light flashed around the crowded chamber. It dazzled in the dark eyes. It smiled a promise on the smiling teeth. And the house of the dead was filled with life.

With a shout of delight the wise-women welcomed the Sun. The old bones glimmered and shimmered. The women began a song to greet the light. Outside the people clapped their hands and beat their drums. They praised the Sun. They rejoiced that the Ancestors were reborn to strength and power.

Meanwhile the Sun soared into the cloudless sky. The last twilight stars winked out. The people sang and danced around the painted house of the Ancestors.

This was the best day of all the long year. Five-Summers-Nearly-Six thought it the best best day of her whole life. She danced with the grown-ups. She pranced and capered with the children from the big houses. She danced among the fires that the men kindled on the pasture. She danced down to the Small Settlement. All day she danced because she was happy. She danced because the Sun had visited the Ancestors. His light made them strong. There was nothing they could not do.

But at last the joyful day came to an end. The feasting was finished. The fires died down. The Midsummer Sun set. The people went to their beds.

For a long time Five-Summers lay awake. She was too excited to sleep. She lay still so that she did not rustle the heather and pine branches that made a sweet springy mattress under the felt sleeping-mat of her bed. But the twigs still rustled. The girl thought a restless vole had made its home in her bed. It was hot too in that Summer night—too hot for sleep. But it was hot in a friendly way, and the girl snuggled into the comfortable cosiness beneath the deerskin and the woollen cloak that covered her.

Next day Five-Summers rose early. She did her chores. She collected water. She milked the two goats who lived in the small house. She made up the fire. She took a bowl of gruel to her grandmother who was old and wise and so always ate breakfast in bed. Then she went out to play.

Five-Summers thought she might call on her cousins in the first big house. But, as she crossed from her own small house, a voice in her ear said, "Hello Five-Summers-Nearly-Six. Are we going to play today?"

She turned quickly. A smiling girl was standing behind her—as though she too had just come from the small house. It was a girl she had never seen before—a girl with fiery orangey-red hair and lips that were made for laughter.

"Hello," said Five-Summers, a little surprised to see a stranger. "Are you new here?"

The stranger girl seemed uncertain for a moment—as though she did not know how to answer. Then her face brightened. "Yes, that's it. I am new."

"Are you staying in one of the big houses? Are you a relative?"

There was a long silence. Then the girl replied hesitantly "... Yes ... No." Another silence. "I am your friend."

Five-Summers began to show her new friend all there was to see in the Small Settlement. But, strangely, the red-haired girl seemed already to know all there was to know. She knew where everyone lived. She knew which women had which husbands—and which were happy and which were not. She knew all the children's names. She even knew the grandparents and the names of babes who had died.

The girls skipped along the field paths that led to the green pasture. The red-haired girl led the way, dancing for joy in the sunshine. She greeted the sheep as though they were old friends. The sheep looked up in surprise, suspicious and edgy, grass in mouth.

The two friends walked down to the white Mothering-Stone among the cornfields. But the new girl seemed afraid of the gleaming boulder. She would not touch its shoulder as all the Small Settlement people did—for a blessing as they passed. And when the red-haired girl drew near to the magic whitestone a little breeze, like a rustling of spirits, stirred the waving corn. Then, for just a moment, Five-Summers felt a pang of fear—the same pang she had felt when she painted the picture on the white cairn-stone.

Five-Summers took her friend to the house of the Ancestors. She wanted to share with her the joyful paintings that covered the big stones. But the red-haired girl hung back. She would not approach the big Ancestor house.

"Come on," called Five-Summers gaily. "Our Ancestors will not harm a friend."

But the girl would not come close. "I cannot," she quavered. "It is dark. It is dark inside. I cannot bear the darkness."

Strange words!

But Five-Summers was too happy to notice. She had a special friend at last! She led the way back to the Small Settlement. "Come and meet my relatives in the big houses," she said.

The red-haired girl looked serious. "They would not want to see me in their houses," she said mysteriously.

"Well, come to the small house. You can share our food. You must speak with my grandmother. Come on!" And Five-Summers ran gaily on ahead. She stopped, breathless, at the door of her small house. She looked round. But her friend was nowhere to be seen. She called out. A skylark shrilled, shouting with delight high overhead, but no friend replied.

Sadly, Five-Summers went into the dim house. All evening she sat moody and silent. Her mother thought she was ill. And the girl snapped rudely at her grandmother who asked what the matter might be. She picked at her food. She was not hungry. At bedtime she left the dish with her uneaten meal at the fireside.

She could not sleep. All night the restless vole rustled her bed. She was hot beneath her woollen cloak. Something seemed to fidget and tickle her feet. She thought the vole had found its way under the covers.

Five-Summers-Nearly-Six rose at dawn. She bustled to finish her chores. She was surprised to find no sign of the meal she had left uneaten the night before. She was dismayed to find the dish broken in pieces. Perhaps some animal had got into the house during the night—a hedgehog or a badger perhaps. Five-Summers brought a bowl of gruel to her grandmother's bedside. The old woman seemed tired and pale. But the girl thought little of it. She was thinking of her new friend.

She went outside. Almost at once the red-haired girl appeared at her elbow.

All day the children chattered and laughed. They sat together beneath a big oak tree that shaded the pasture. But it was strange. The red-haired girl never asked a question. She knew already all about Five-Summers, her life, her family and even her most secret thoughts. She knew other things too—secret things. She was as clever almost as a careful mother; as wise almost as a grandmother.

The day passed in a flash. The long Summer day was too short for all the girlish chatter that Five-Summers had in her head. All of a sudden it was evening—time to go home.

"Do come back to the small house," Five-Summers begged.

But her friend was reluctant.

Five-Summers tried to persuade her. "You must meet my mother. You will like my grandmother."

"But your grandmother will not like me," replied the girl mysteriously.

"I do think you're afraid!" Five-Summers teased. "You mustn't fear Grandmother. She's a bit strange—but that's just the magic in her. She sees things of which she never speaks. And she talks to the Ancestors."

"I know," murmured the red-haired girl. "I know and so I will not come."

"If you don't come, I shall think you don't like me," Five-Summers pouted.

"But surely real friends can feel close even when they are apart?" replied the red-haired girl. Her voice was wise—much wiser than it should have been.

And then she was gone.

Five-Summers went home alone. Her mother was waiting, an anxious frown on her face. She did not mention the broken dish. She was more concerned about Grandmother. The old wise-woman was tired and listless. All day she had sat on her stool by the hearth. She had eaten nothing and drunk only a sip of herb tea. All day she had stared into the fire and muttered in the old-fashioned words that wise-women used to speak with the Ancestors. Then she had shuffled to her bed where she now lay staring into space—her lips moving, but saying nothing.

The small-house family ate its evening meal in silence and went to bed early.

Five-Summers was tired after her long day with her red-haired friend. But she did not sleep soundly. Her dreams were filled with her friend's voice. The naughty vole rustled in her bed like a restless spirit. And she was too warm under the covers—as though she was hugged in a hot cuddle all night long.

Next day Grandmother did not leave her bed. She drank a little herb tea. She grumbled at the bitter medicine that Five-Summers helped her mother to prepare.

Five-Summers-Nearly-Six went out to play with her new friend. She spoke of her grandmother's illness. But the red-haired girl shrugged as though she did not care. Then she took her friend by the hand and together the girls skipped along the field paths to the woodland edge. All day they talked and played. And Five-Summers never thought once about her grandmother whose sickness cast a cloud over the small house.

Again at night Five-Summers was troubled by dreams. Next morning her grandmother was even more pale and poorly. The old woman lay in her bed. She chanted a song. It was not a magic spell for healing. It was a charm against evil— a secret spell used only for the most powerful magic. The mother and father of the small house were anxious and quietly fearful. Perhaps Grandmother would die. Five-Summers-Nearly-Six went out to play.

And so the long warm days passed. But for each day that Five-Summers spent with her red-haired friend, Grandmother grew a little weaker.

The two friends played wonderful games. They went deep into the forest. The red-haired girl knew every path and every secret place. When Five-Summers was afraid in the green and leafy darkness, her friend took her hand and the fear floated away. "No forest spirit can harm you," said the red-haired girl. "No wolf or bear, no bristling boar or angry aurochs (fierce wild bull of the forest) will dare come near if I am with you."

They played hide-and-seek. But somehow Five-Summers could never stay hidden for long. However carefully she hid—however quiet she was—she would turn and there was the red-haired girl at her side. But when the red-haired girl went to hide she seemed to melt into the air. She seemed to become invisible—as dark as the rough-barked trees, as cold as the rocks that shouldered up from the mossy earth.

The girls swam in the clear pool beneath a rushing waterfall. The red-haired girl dived from a high rock. She flashed through the air like a kingfisher—sharp as a sliver of sky. She leaped in the water like a fish—quick as the crystal light. When she lay on the grassy bank her red hair spread in a fiery web as though it were not wet at all.

So the Summer passed. The girls played. Grandmother lay in her bed, muttering magic. And strange things happened in the small-house. There was the broken dish. Other dishes and bowls were mysteriously broken too. Food was spoiled. A big water pot shattered in the night and water gushed hissing into the hearth: a hearthstone cracked and the fire was drowned. A grain-sack split and seed-corn for the Spring spilled onto the floor. The greedy goats broke their tethers and ate the corn. A wooden milk pail toppled from its shelf and the cream saved for butter-making drained away into the earthen floor of the small house like an offering to the Ancestors.

Sometimes the small house door blew open, though there was no wind. One night a storm battered the Small Settlement. The big houses were undamaged, but the small house creaked and cracked. It groaned as if in pain. A roof timber snapped. Father clambered up a ladder to repair it. As he worked he cut his hand. Drops of blood fell into the fire. They boiled and bubbled. Mother's skill seemed to desert her. The weaving went wrong. Threads snapped and the cloth was spoiled. New-made pots shattered in the fire. The butter would not come. The salt was damp. Sheep fell sick. Cattle became lame. And all the clever mother's medicine could not cure them.

Grandmother was very sick now. She muttered, "An Ancestor is restless. She eats our food. She takes our strength to feed her life."

The wise-women came from the big houses. But they shook their heads and would not cross the threshold of the small house. They chanted spells from the doorway. Then they departed. They said the small house grandmother must die. She had the smell of the Ancestors upon her.

The small house grew sad and fearful. Spirits were at work. Grandmother was wise and old—but it was not yet her time to join the Ancestors.

At last, Grandmother begged to be taken to the house of the Ancestors. Father helped her to walk up to the big pale stone house that overlooked the Small Settlement. He watched as the old woman crept inside. For a day and a night Grandmother remained alone with the Ancestors. For a night and a day she chanted alone in the darkness. Mother took food to her. She returned saying that the old wise-woman now knew how her sickness had come about. But only the girl Five-Summers-Nearly-Six could help her find a cure.

Five-Summers crept into the dim chamber of the Ancestor house. Grandmother was seated on a little stool. The skulls of the Ancestors, who usually smiled, seemed to scowl in the feeble flickering lamplight. Grandmother was pale, but her eyes were as bright as the edge of a black flint knife. She mumbled a magic charm. In her hand she held a small brown skull. At her side was a big chunk of magic whitestone. She rubbed the stone with a whitestone pebble. A cool yellow glow lit up the stone. It lit up the picture of a little girl—all orangey-red, with orangey red plaits and an orangey-red skirt and orangey-red bangles on her orangey-red arms and ankles. Five-Summers-Nearly-Six was filled with fear.

"Come in my dear," whispered Grandmother in a kindly voice. "And will your friend not join us too?"

Five-Summers spun round. The red-haired girl was at her shoulder.

Drawn into Grandmother's spell the two friends sat together in the lamplight. The Ancestors watched. At last Grandmother spoke. She spoke to the red-haired girl.

"Ah! At last we meet properly. I can see you clearly here in your own house. You were always hiding when I glimpsed you in my own small house. But I saw you when you ate young Five-Summers's food. I saw you break the dish. I saw you nestle against her in her bed at night. I was watching when you spilled the milk and slit the grain-sack. I saw you quench the fire and crack the roof-beam. I watched while you took strength from the cattle and the sheep. I saw you drink the blood of the small-house father."

The red-haired girl tried to speak, but no words came from her mouth.

Five-Summers's heart beat loudly. The sound filled her ears and made her head swim. There was great magic here.

"So tell me, my dear," Grandmother continued, "who are you and what do you want from us?"

The red-haired girl spoke in the old-fashioned voice that the wise-women used. "I am an Ancestor," she said.

"I know that," said Grandmother. She was stern—but not unkind. "But why do you come among us in this form?"

The girl glanced at the painted stone. "I come because I was called. I come to be a friend to the lonely girl."

"But when an Ancestor takes a human shape it steals strength from the living."

"I know, and I am sorry for it," replied the red-haired spirit girl. "But I did so much want to live in the world again—just for a season—and to have a friend to laugh with in the sunshine."

"But you had a life before you joined the Ancestors."

"Oh! But it was too short," the spirit girl cried.

"Tell me of your life," said the old woman gently.

"I came with my mother from beyond the salt sea. We came in our big boats. We brought our sheep and cattle and our seed-corn and our black axes. The men felled the forest. The women planted the fields. But the wildmen came in the night. They trampled our corn. They killed our goats with their wasp-sharp arrows. They stole the young girls out of the houses." Tears sprang in the eyes of the red-haired girl. "I was taken. But I escaped. I ran and ran. The wildmen chased me. I came to some rocks. The wildmen threw their spears. I fell ..."

Grandmother patted the girl's hand. She looked to her granddaughter. "Now then, Five-Summers-Nearly-Six. You made a wish and a promise. Your picture cast a spell. Now you must make a choice. You must choose between your grandmother and your friend. If your friend is to live in the world, I must take her place among the Ancestors."

"But you must not die, grandmother!" Five-Summers sobbed.

"We all must die one day—a moment of sleep so we may wake and live forever with the Ancestors."

"But it is not yet your time." She turned to her friend. "I am so sorry. My grandmother is the thing I love most in all the world."

"But you made a promise," said the red-haired girl crossly. "Promises must be kept."

"Then let *me* live with the Ancestors—so Grandmother can be well again."

"The red-haired girl smiled sadly. Now she spoke like a grown-up. "That was well said, young Five-Summers-Nearly-Six. Those were brave wise words. I cannot keep you to your promise."

"The Ancestors are generous and wise," murmured the old woman.

Grandmother placed the whitestone in her granddaughter's hand. "Our Law forbids us to paint any picture—and now you know why. The power of the Ancestors is strong. The picture comes alive and it takes life from the world."

Five-Summers wept. She wept because her selfish promise had made her grandmother sick. She wept because she had acted like a thoughtless little child of just five summers. She wept for the shortness of her friend's life. And she wept because she had broken the great Law of her people. A tear fell onto the painted stone. The red-paint smudged. The red-haired girl smiled. Her fiery hair shimmered in the lamplight. Another tear fell and another. The paint smeared. The red-haired girl began to fade like mist on the morning meadow.

A tear fell onto the painted stone.

"Goodbye my friend who gave me a season of life in the world. Remember me. I shall be with you always."

Another tear fell and she was gone.

Grandmother rose to her feet. She placed the small brown skull gently on a shelf. She stroked it as though she were smoothing the hair of a small child. "It is done," she said. "The spell is broken. All is as it should be. All is well." She took her granddaughter's small hand and gave it a friendly squeeze. "Now Five-Summers-Nearly-Six, you may take me home."

And from that moment all was well in the small house. Grandmother was as round and rosy as if she had never been ill. Five-Summers-Nearly-Six had learned a great lesson and loved her grandmother more than ever. Grandmother said the girl would be a great wise-woman when she grew up—because she had lived for a season with the Ancestors. Five-Summers was glad that her grandmother was well again, though she was sad for the red-haired girl. But she knew her spirit-friend was watching over her. She knew that real friends can feel close even when they are apart. And one day—after many many Summers had passed—they would meet again in the dim house of the Ancestors.

And so all was well and the world was a joyful place. The Sun shone. The corn grew high and the cattle grew fat. The sheep's wool was finer and their milk sweeter than ever before. A year passed—and another Midsummer festival. The power of the Ancestors was renewed. And a baby came to the mother of the small house: a baby girl who would be a sister and a friend to Five-Summers-Nearly-Six (who was now nine Summers old and nearly a grown-up) and live with her in the small-house.

Five-Summers-Nearly-Six gazed in wonder at the newborn. Her new sister lay on a soft fleece. She was as rose-petal pink as the pale blushed whitestone pebbles that lay on the house of the Ancestors. She was perfect. She had perfect tiny toes and perfect fingers and impossibly tiny perfect fingernails. Her perfect blue eyes shone like little glimpses of the sky. And her happy face was framed by a perfect glowing downy halo of brilliant orangey-red hair.

She was perfect.

CHAPTER 5

▼

THE MAKING OF THE KING

Long long ago, the second age of people in the land was a time of peace and plenty.

The men (who were the fathers of us all) cut down the forests. They felled the trees with axes of black stone and polished flint. They burned the brambly thickets. When the fires died away they ploughed the ashy earth to make fields and gardens.

Then the women came. The women (who were the mothers of us all) came with their rakes of deer antler and their hoes. They planted seeds of corn. They sang magic songs to make the wheat and barley grow.

The men built sturdy wooden houses for their wives and children. They built their houses from the stout trunks and branches of the forest trees. The walls were of woven wattle daubed with clay. The roofs were covered with a thatch of corn-field straw and sedges pulled from the boggy places.

The women gathered their corn at the Summer's end. They ground their flour on the rough grinding-stones at their firesides. They made bread and porridge and plump dumplings for their husbands and their children.

The careful women combed wool from the backs of the sheep and goats that grazed the hillsides and the forest edge. The skilful women wove the wool into warm cloth. They stitched the cloth. They made skirts and coats and winter cloaks to wear with warm felt and fur in Winter.

The clever women made strong pots of clay. In the pots they stored their salt. And in the pots they cooked food for their husbands and their children

The busy women gathered straw and willow withies. They plaited baskets for their corn. They made baskets in which to store their Winter clothes through the Summer days. They used baskets to carry the fruits and Autumn mushrooms, and the hazel nuts they gathered in the woodland. They used their baskets to carry the gleaming fish they caught in the lakes and rivers.

The wise women made magic spells and secret potions. With powerful charms and wordless wisdom they protected their families. They healed the men when they were hurt at work or in their hunting. With herbs and medicines they cured their children when they were sick. They cursed their enemies until they withered and died.

The women sang the songs that remembered the story of their people. They spoke mysterious words. They sang to the spirits of the Earth and Water. They spoke to the spirits of the Ancestors whose dry brown bones lay in the great stone house on the hill.

The spirits heard the magic songs and they caused the corn to sprout. They made the lambs that played upon the pasture. They made the bleating kids that frisked beside the nanny goats on the hillside. They made the curious calves that nuzzled against the wide-eyed cows in the damp meadow. The spirits brought sweet milk to the cows and goats and sheep, which the clever women made into pale butter and creamy cheese.

The spirits of the Ancestors guided the ploughs of the men. They spoke with the spirits of Earth and Water. The Ancestors lent their ancient power to the strong women (who were the mothers of us all) as they worked in the fields. They taught them the secrets of the growing corn. They taught them how their babies came. The Ancestors guided the hands of the clever women as they shaped their pots and plaited their baskets and wove their woollen cloth. They watched over the people in the darkness. They feasted by the firesides in the big wooden houses while the family slept. And they threaded through the dreaming of children.

The Spirits of the Ancestors threaded through the dreaming of children.

For many many lifetimes the people prospered. Fields and gardens covered the land. Cattle, sheep and goats grazed every waterside meadow and every windy mountain. There were big wooden houses in every valley. And when the men and women (who were the fathers and mothers of us all) grew old, they went happily to sleep and dream forever in the big stone house on the hillside. They joined the Ancestors to watch over the men and women who were their children (and who were the fathers and mothers of us all).

In those long long-ago days of our second age, the Sun and Moon (who were the father and the mother of all the world) lived, it is said, close to the men and women (who were the fathers and mothers of us all).

Each day, it is said, the Sun swam through the clear air. He glanced into each big wooden house to wake the people. He visited each field and garden. His touch awakened his daughter, the Earth, in Spring. His smile made the green corn turn to gold. Once in each year—at Midsummer or Midwinter—the Sun reached into the house of the Ancestors. He warmed the old brown bones as they lay in the gloom. He put light into their dark eyes. He gave them life and power, and they grew strong in their deep dreaming.

At night the Sun hid his face. He went away, it was said, to warm the houses and gardens of tribes who lived in a land of valleys beneath the far-away mountains.

Then his wife, the soft round Moon, kissed her light upon her daughter, the Earth, who slumbered all clothed in flocks and crops. The Moon whispered soft words into the ears of the waving corn. She quieted the silly bleating of the fearful sheep. The motherly Moon smiled on the sleep of the men and women (who were the fathers and mothers of us all).

She quieted the silly bleating of the fearful sheep.

Now and then she crept into the house of the Ancestors to watch their dreams for a while. She shone upon the spirits of the Ancestors as they wandered from their great stone house on the hillside. She watched the spirits as they fed on the food folk left for them by the firesides. She saw the mysterious Ancestors as they guarded the crops from wicked spirits or protected the flocks from foxes and wolves. She saw the spirits of the Ancestors as they flittered among the dreams of the people (who were their children—and the fathers and mothers of us all), filling their thoughts with wisdom and mischief.

For many many lifetimes all was well. But as the people prospered they grew proud. As the Ancestors grew in power they became scornful of the Sun and Moon (who were the father and the mother of all the world). The Ancestors visited the dreams of the women (who were the mothers of us all). They filled the cunning women with wicked thoughts.

The women spoke among themselves. They met at the firesides of the big wooden houses. They whispered one to another in the fields and at their weaving looms. They murmured together as they watched the burning fires that hardened the clay of their pots.

The men worked all day and all night.

"We are strong," they said. "We are strong in our bodies. We are strong in skill. We are strong in our husbands who have felled the forest and who plough the fields and build our big wooden houses."

"We are strong," the women said, "in many mysteries. We are strong in wisdom and in magic. We are strong in the power of the Ancestors."

Then the women (who were the mothers of us all) called to their husbands.

"Come," they said. "Come with your strong backs and your oxen. Come with your black axes and your wooden spades. Come with your antler picks and your ox-shoulder shovels. Come to do the work we have planned. Come to a work that shall be the greatest thing in all the world. It shall be a greater work than the raising of the stones of the Ancestors' house. It shall be greater than the piling of the cairn that covers the house of the Ancestors."

Then the women set their men to work. They set them to work to build a high place in the land. They told the men to gather stones and heap up mounds of earth. So the men began to gather stones and heap up piles of earth.

The men worked all day and all night. They worked under the heat of the sun and in the cool of the moonlight until their high place over-topped the big wooden houses. It towered over the tallest stone house of the Ancestors.

The women urged on the men. The spirits of the Ancestors taught the women a magic spell to make their men work day and night and never tire. The women brewed a potion that drove sleep from the eyes of the men and gave them strength. And so, by little and little, the high place grew tall. It towered over the forest trees. It scraped its top against the sky.

Then the women cried, "Enough!"

Now they called upon the strongest of their husbands. They gave them magic charms to drive away fear. They called upon the fiercest hunters from among their husbands. They gave them potions to give them strength. Then they armed their men. They gave them stiff new bows with strings of sinew twisted with the Ancestor's power. They gave them flint-bladed spears and arrows—all new with leaf-sharp flint tips. They gave them flawless black stone axes, whose edges were honed by a moontime of grinding on the stones of the Ancestors' house. They gave to their menfolk, nets of knotted charms and ropes of twisted magic.

"Now all is ready," said the women (who were the mothers of us all). "Now our men who are as brave and strong as flesh and blood can be, shall go to the high place that scrapes the sky. They shall go to the high place with their spears and bows, their leaf-sharp flint-tipped arrows. They shall go with their glossy black axes and their nets and ropes."

The men (who were the fathers of us all) obeyed their women. They climbed to the top of the high place with their weapons and their nets. When they stood on the top of the high place, they said to one another, "Why are we here? What is it we are to do?"

Their wives called from below, "You will catch the Sun as he passes. You will stab him with your flint-bladed spears—as you would stab the fierce fat boar or the fleet deer of the forest. You will loose your leaf-sharp arrows at the Sun to wound him—as you pierce the wings of the flying geese."

"The wounded Sun will falter in his course across the sky," the women cried. "Then you will stun him with your black axes. You will catch him in your strong nets. You will bind him with your twisted ropes."

The men were doubtful. But they were not afraid because of the magic spell their wives had made. Nor would they dare to disobey the women who were so full of magic power and mysteries—the women who were their loving wives (and who were the mothers of us all).

While the men waited for the Sun to pass by, the women made their plans. They planned to charm the captive sun with magic spells. They planned to tether the enchanted Sun among their field and gardens like a milking goat. Then it would be bright and light all day and night in the fields and gardens. All day and all year the Sun would make the corn grow. There would be no night and no Wintertime.

The women planned to make the Sun their slave. He would do their work. He would sharpen the axes of the men until they were as keen as his own bright light. He would harden the women's pots so they would never break in the fire. He would make the men stronger than the wind among the forest trees. He would make the women's magic sharper than the whitest salt.

The women of that long, long-ago time were fierce in their power. The women (who were the mothers of us all) were terrible in their thirst for knowledge.

They sang, "We shall take a basketful of sunshine every day into the house of the Ancestors. The Sun will warm their old brown bones every morning—not just once a year. The life of the spirits in the great stone house will be renewed each day. The power of the Ancestors will grow and grow."

The women sang their song. "The Ancestors in their power will teach us every secret. They will unlock every mystery. Then, like the Moon (who is the mother of all the world) we shall know how life is made."

But even while the women plotted to enslave the Sun, one man thought that this was wrong. He was a good man. He was not rich in cattle or fields. But he was quiet and thoughtful. His wives and sons and daughters obeyed him as the head of his family. And his small wooden house was peaceful and happy.

This one good man did not help to build the high place that touched the sky. His wives did not join in the song of the fierce women. The good man's wives were quiet and content with their own wisdom as they sowed their wheat in the field and ground their flour at the fireside. They were happy to shape their pots and cook food for their husband and children.

The one good man spoke to the Moon as she looked into his house at night. He told her what the fierce women planned. He warned her of the men who lay in wait with spears and arrows, axes, magic nets and strong ropes. But the Moon—who sees into the hearts of all living things because she lives in the dreaming world of darkness—knew of the cunning women's plans. She kindly thanked the good man for his warning.

"I have seen all the things of which you speak," said the shining Moon. "I have seen the women become ambitious. I have seen the spirits of the Ancestors grow in power. I have seen the men who lie in wait. My husband the Sun too has seen these things. And my husband knows how to break the hearts of the Ancestors. He knows how to punish his wilful children."

Then the good man became afraid. "Shall I be punished too?" he asked.

The Moon replied, "As the women sow the corn, so they reap the golden harvest. The men may fell the forest tree, but they cannot make it grow again. The women shape their clay. They bake their pots in the fire. But they cannot reshape the clay—until the pot is smashed and returned to the earth."

The fearful man asked, "Why must I be punished too? Must every pot be broken because some are cracked in the fire? Must the lamb be killed because the ewe is sick?"

The Moon heard the man's plea. His words were wise. The Moon was thoughtful but said nothing. She spoke to her husband the Sun. But he swore a great and angry oath. He told his wife to hold her tongue. He said that not one of the troublesome humans would escape his anger.

Then the Sun called his sons. He had sired seven thousand sons. Seven thousand came to their father's call. Each was clad in a grey fleece cloak. The sky filled with clouds and the day grew dark.

Each of the seven thousand carried a stiff tall bow and a never-emptying quiver of arrows. The bows were the lightning. The arrows were the rain. Seven thousand sons shouted their father's anger in seven thousand thunderclaps. They shot their arrows onto the world of the men and women (who were the fathers and mothers of us all).

The bows were the lightning. The arrows were the rain.

The world began to fill with water. The rivers rushed through their valleys washing away the crops and flocks and the big wooden houses. The lakes and pools filled and overflowed, flooding the pastures. The waters lapped up the flanks of the high place.

"Oh help me!" cried the good man as the waters swelled to flood the whole world. "Save me! Save my corn and my cattle! Save my sons and my sheep! Save my dainty goats and my wives and daughters!"

The gentle Moon heard the good man's cries. She took pity on him because he was not to blame for the wickedness of the cunning women. The salt-white sparkling moon reached down from the sky. She cupped her hand into a little sickle-slender boat. She scooped the good man from the earth. She scooped up the man and his wives, and his sons and his daughters, and all his animals, and his fields, and his crops and his small wooden house. Then the good man and all he possessed sailed high among the stars in the shining boat of the Moon.

The Moon held her chosen one safe until the anger of her husband, the Sun, died away. Then all of her seven thousand sons put off their grey fleece cloaks. They returned their arrows of rain and hail back to their never-emptying quivers. Then the Sun shone again and the Earth rose out of the clean waters all rosy, round and refreshed.

He spoke to him at Midsummer

The gentle Moon put her good man back on the Earth. She returned him safely with his animals and his crops, his house and his wives, and his sons and his daughters. Then the Moon kissed her husband, the Sun. Now he was sorry that he had drowned the whole world. He was grateful to his wife, the Moon, for saving one man to begin the world again. And as a token, he gave the gentle Moon a marvellous necklace. She held it in the air. It glittered like the blood-red garnet. It glowed like the orange and the honey-yellow amber. It gleamed like the green stone that melts in fire to make the sun-bright copper. It glistered like the blue glass that men make from the melting of sand.

The Sun was dismayed by the pride of the men and women (who were the fathers and mothers of us all). He moved far from the earth. He refused now to speak to all the people of the world. He would never again speak to women. He spoke only to the one good man. He spoke to him at Midsummer in a place the good man made. It was a circle of stones within an earthen bank, which only the one good man (the servant of the Sun) might enter. And the wisdom and the power of the Sun were not now given to all. It was not given to the Ancestors. It was a secret from the women. This wisdom now came only to the one good man whom the people called a King. And so the one good man was the first King in the world.

In later times men remembered the great flood. They blamed the wicked women. And so they never again allowed their wives to become so powerful or wise. They blamed the spirits of the Ancestors. And so they shut up the great stone houses where the old brown bones were laid. The Ancestors, who had been drowned in the waters, were now hidden from the Sun. They withered and shrank into spiteful fairy folk who tempted and teased and tormented the good people of the world.

The Sun and Moon gave signs to the good man so that he—and all his sons and grandsons and their wives (who were the fathers and mothers of us all)—would never forget the first great flood.

The kindly Moon reminded the people of how she had saved the good man. She made a great stone—as white as moon-shine, as round as the mothering earth—to grow from the good ground. She sailed the sign of her silver boat in the sky. And now and then too she showed her necklace to the people. Then they knew that the rain fell as a gentle blessing, not the wrath of gods.

But the Sun did not forget the wickedness of the people in the long long-ago time. And now and then he reminded the world of what he had done—and what he might do again. So sometimes he hid his face to make the sky dark in the day-time. And he scattered sunshine-yellow gold among the rocks and rivers for the people to find. This was a sign that the Sun—who now sailed high in the sky, far out of reach—had once, long long ago, lived close to the people of the Earth.

The people gave the gold they found to their Kings. And the Kings ruled in the world with the wisdom of the Sun for seventy generations. And each King, when he died, was laid in the arms of the Earth in a high place where the Sun would know who he was. And each King, after he died, was taken up in the silver boat of the Moon. He sailed among the stars. And he lived in the gilded house of the Sun forever.

The silver boat of the Moon.

CHAPTER 6

▼

THE CRAFTSMAN'S REWARD

The Craftsman sat at the door of his workshop. He had worked all morning striking flakes from a big lump of chalky-skinned black flint. He had worked all afternoon shaping the flakes into different sorts of tool. There were scrapers for cleaning animal skins. There were knives and spear points, woodworking blades and barbed arrowheads. Tomorrow the Craftsmen would finish the tools. Some he would mount in a handle. Some he would fit with a leather handgrip. All would be given an edge as sharp as an adder's bite.

Now, in the evening, the Craftsman rested his keen eyes and his clever hands. He sat by the door of his workshop. He had done a good day's work and he was a contented man.

He had every reason to be happy. He sat watching the Sun set while he counted his blessings. He was the wealthiest man in the whole valley—except of course for the King. The Craftsman gazed across to the hillside where the cattle of the whole valley grazed. Among the herd were the scores of beasts that bore his brand. Only the King owned more cattle—and that was as it should be. The Craftsman's contented eye followed the ripples that flowed across the ripening barley. The crop in his own fields stood taller and more golden than any of his neighbours' corn. Only the King's fields were more fertile—and that too was as it should be.

The Craftsman's workshop stood in one corner of a large enclosure. The walls of the Craftsman's place were of neatly laid boulders and stones cleared from the fields. The walls stood to shoulder height in a broad oval. Only the King's walls rose higher.

Within the Craftsman's enclosure, several garden plots were green with herbs and vegetables. These were cared for by the Craftsman's careful younger daughter.

The Craftsman's house—like his workshop—was a sturdy round stone-walled building with a tall conical thatched roof. Wisps of smoke and teasing aromas leaked from the eaves. The Craftsman's wife was making bread to mop up the evening meal of beef stew with greens and dumplings. His favourite!

In a smaller round house lived the Craftsman's first daughter. She was married to a rather slow dull young man from the next valley. Unusually, he had chosen to live in the shadow of his wife's father instead of taking his bride away to live in his own place. The Craftsman was far richer than his own people—so perhaps he was not so stupid after all. And in five years his young wife had given him three healthy children—so perhaps he was not so dull either.

A third round house belonged to the Craftsman's two sons. They were big hearty boys of sixteen and eighteen Summers—grown men, in fact, but not yet married. They needed their own house. They kept a slave girl who looked after them. She washed their clothes and made their bread and cleaned their house. She probably had other duties too. But the Craftsman did not interfere.

He was proud of his sons. His first son was a herdsman. He was a skilful stock-man—a good judge of livestock and a canny trader. Under his management the Craftsman's cattle increased. And only the King's beasts yielded softer wool or richer milk or sweeter meat.

The Craftsman's younger son had learned his father's skills. He could cast bronze and work with wood and bone. He could knap flints almost as well as his father.

He could cast bronze

And so the Craftsman was a contented man. His sons were admired. His daughters were quiet. His wife was fine and round and rosy. He thought of her, crouched over the fire in his big house, stirring a pot and happy to be making her husband's supper. She was a woman who spoke little and never nagged or scolded. She did her work without complaint. She could shape a fair clay pot and weave good woollen cloth. She knew medicine and herbs and had made four fine babies. She was a perfect wife.

The workshop was the Craftsman's favourite place. He spent most of his daylight time here. Few people had seen inside the workshop. Foolish and jealous folk said there was magic inside. The Craftsman smiled at this. But he never said there was no magic in the smoky round house. The threat of magic kept nosy folk away. He did not want idle eyes watching him nor idle tongues distracting him while he worked. He did not want careless hands touching his tools. He did not want anyone to learn of the secret place under the flat stone by the hearth where he kept a hoard of flint and bronze.

Of course there was magic in the Craftsman. His hands were blessed by the Gods with gifts of skill. And his heart was blessed with a quiet wisdom and a canny knack for accumulating wealth.

The Craftsman kept no slaves. His strong sons and his daughter's husband were usually all the help he needed. Nonetheless, he looked out for neighbours who had fallen on hard times—because their cattle were sick or their wives lazy. Then he offered them work in his fields or around his workshop. In return he gave them meat and bread, or a goat or seed-corn. He gave far more in food than he received in work. But the Craftsman was happy to share his wealth with neighbours.

The Craftsman lived a quiet life. He drank the beer his wife brewed. But he had never been drunk. He enjoyed the food his wife cooked. But he never grew fat. He welcomed the good things his wealth brought—warm clothes, a big house, trade goods such as jet and amber beads. But he was not vain.

Neighbours came to the Craftsman's fireside. They sought advice concerning sick cattle, disobedient wives and the marriage of children. These tricky matters should really have been decided by the King. After all, the King spoke with the Gods, and so his judgement a special thing. But the Craftsman's commonsense was almost as good as the King's divine wisdom. And the Craftsman did not demand a gift when giving guidance.

The King might have objected to the Craftsman's impertinence in giving free advice to his people. But the King was old, and he was also the Craftsman's friend. He was happy that a friend should take some of the burden of kingship from his shoulders.

During the long Winter evenings, the Craftsman would sit in the big round house of his friend, the King. The King's house was very grand. It was larger even than the Craftsman's home. It was cosier too. The stone walls were lined with wattle and hung with skins, fleeces and woollen cloth. The King's fire never smoked and a slave brought dry logs whenever it burned down.

The Craftsman enjoyed the King's good beer. And he was not jealous that the King drank from a glorious golden cup while he drank from a coarse pottery beaker. This was just as it should be.

The King was old enough to have been the Craftsman's father. Yet he treated him (almost) as an equal. He liked the Craftsman's company and conversation. The two men spoke of their cattle and their sheep. They spoke of the harvest. They discussed the problems that arose between neighbours in the broad valley that was the King's realm.

Sometimes the King spoke of his wives. Then his voice fell to a whisper. He was rather afraid of those two lean fierce women who stopped quarrelling with each other only when they joined forces to scold their husband. The craftsman listened quietly to his old friend's whispered words and gave what comfort he could. Inside his own belly, though, the Craftsman felt warm and content because his own round rosy wife was never troublesome.

The King sometimes spoke of his own two sons. Then he sighed sadly. They were the same age as the Craftsman's boys. But they were very different from the Craftsman's bright honest lads. The King's first son was powerful and fearless— but a loud bullying brute. He cared for nothing but fighting and hunting. The King's younger son was soft and handsome—but a vain strutting capercailzie cock. He thought of nothing but his beads and bangles and his slave girls. The Craftsman gave the old King what comfort he could, but felt his heart swell with pride because his own two sons were bold and honest, gentle, skilful and strong.

Sometimes the King sought the Craftsman's advice on matters which the Gods alone should decide. One day the old King even asked his friend to say which of his sons should be king when he went to live with the Gods. The Craftsman did not answer. He knew—and the old King knew too—that neither was worthy. Once the King murmured over the rim of his golden cup, "If only you had been my son." Then the Craftsman was silent and thoughtful.

Of course, the King was a king, and so the Craftsman was always respectful. Even when the King spoke to his friend as if to a son or younger brother, the Craftsman replied in words proper for a king. Because a king was not like ordinary men. He alone could make the offering of milk and corn at the round white mothering-stone among the cornfields. He alone could make the sacrifice of the slanting father-of-stone on the pasture. And he alone went into the Midsummer circle of great stones. He spoke to the Gods. He alone heard the voice of the Sun. In his long life the old King had three times received the wisdom of the Moon that came only once in nineteen Summers. The King was, in part, a God. And so the Craftsman was more respectful than if his friend were an ordinary man.

But the Craftsman did not respect the King's sons. He despised them. He despised them for what they were. He despised them for their high-handed treatment of the valley folk. He despised them for secret reasons of his own.

One day, the King's first son came to the Craftsman's place. He strode up to the workshop and cried, "Ho! Craftsman!" in his loud bully's voice. He did not wait for a reply. He barged into the workshop.

The Craftsman looked up from his work—a beautiful carved bone pin. He stared into the brutal bearded face that blocked out the light.

"Put that away," said the King's son. "I've got more important work for you— work that I want done—and I want it quick too."

"I am always happy to help the son of my friend—the first son of the King," said the Craftsman politely. "What may I do for you?"

"I want a new axe. I want it big. I want it hafted. I want it sharp. I want it decorated. And I want it before the Moon is full again."

He did not say 'please'.

He barged into the workshop

"A bronze axe is a large task," said the Craftsman in a quiet voice. "I am happy to do the work. But what will you give me for the bronze I use, for the charcoal that fuels the furnace, and for the time and skill that will belong to your axe?"

"I'll give you ..." A nasty gleam came into the big bully's eye. A fierce grin twisted his bearded face. "You shall have a freshly killed deer every new moon for a whole year."

Thirteen deer was a good price.

"They must be antlered stags," said the Craftsman.

"Stags if you like," agreed the first son, "and if you do the work well."

And then he was gone.

The Craftsman did the work well. He spent a whole quarter-moon carving a stone mould for the big axe. He used his whole stock of bronze. He used a score of baskets of charcoal to heat the furnace to melt the metal. When the axe was cool, he spent two days finishing it, and another quarter-moon chipping zigzag patterns onto the blade. He spent a whole day carving the ash handle; another day binding the leather handgrip; two days more honing the edge and polishing the best axe in all the world until it shone like dawn sunlight.

The King's son returned to collect his axe. He peered at the patterned blade. He turned it over in his hand and felt the keen edge with his grubby thumb. He hefted it to feel its weight. He grinned a bearded bully's grin.

"It's a good axe," he said at last.

"It is a good axe," the Craftsman agreed. "It is well worth the price of thirteen antlered stags. When will you bring the first of them?"

The King's son laughed. It was a big boorish guffaw of a laugh.

"I never said I'd bring any such thing." And with that he pressed a single arrowhead into the Craftsman's hand.

The Craftsman looked at the flint. It was a poor thing—lop-sided, blunt and with a broken tip. It was not an arrowhead from his workshop.

"What is the meaning of this?" he asked.

The King's son laughed again. "Why, that's your thirteen stags. Just get yourself a bow, make a shaft for the arrowhead, and you can shoot your thirteen stags—or as many more as you please."

And with that he walked, laughing loudly, out of the workshop.

The Craftsman flung the arrowhead into the workshop fire. It glowed red and cracked in the flames. The Craftsman called on all the Gods of the earth and the sky to give him revenge on this loud bully who had cheated him. He would not tell the King. He would trust the Gods and bide his time.

Some time later the King's younger son came to the Craftsman's workshop. He came with a tinkling and a jingling of bangles and beads. He did not call out. He sidled into the workshop without a word.

The Craftsman looked up from his work—a flint-bladed knife in a carved wooden handle. He looked at the smooth-cheeked face that seemed to sneer in the lamplight.

"Put that away," said the King's son. "I've got more important work for you— work that I want done—and I want it done quick."

"I am always happy to help the son of my friend—the second son of the King," said the Craftsman politely. "What may I do for you?"

"I want hair ornaments. I want a pair of them. I want them in gold. I want them decorated. I want them for the feast of the Autumn Moon."

He did not say 'please'.

"Gold ornaments are not easy work," said the Craftsman in his quiet voice. "I am happy to do the work. But what will you give me for the gold I must find, for the special tools I must make for this task, for the time and skill that will belong to your ornaments?"

"I'll give you ..." A sly glint shone in the second son's eyes. A sneak's smile spread across his girlish lips. "You shall have a whole field of corn each year for seven years."

Seven harvests was a good price.

"It must be wheat, not barley," said the Craftsman.

"Wheat if you like," agreed the second son, "and if you do the work well."

And then he was gone.

The Craftsman did the work well. He traded his best beasts—bulls and fat cows—for the gold he needed. His son took the cattle to the trading place and returned with a tiny bag of gold dust. The craftsman put the dust into a pot of clay. He melted the gold in his furnace fire. He made two beads of gold. He beat them flat and thin as a fish-scale. Then he shaped two identical ornaments. He decorated them with patterns of tiny punched marks. He bent them into shape.

At harvest time the King's son returned to collect his ornaments. He held them so that they glinted in the sunlight. He weighed them in his hand. He stroked them with his slender fingers. He bound them in the chinkling ringlets of his hair.

"They're fine ornaments," said the King's son.

He bound them in the chinkling ringlets of his hair.

"They are fine ornaments indeed," agreed the Craftsman, "well worth the price of seven harvests. I look forward to the first load of grain being brought to me now it is the Summer's end."

The King's son laughed. It was a shrill jackdaw's cackle of a laugh.

"I never said I'd bring any such thing." And with that he pressed a small fistful of corn into the Craftsman's hand.

The Craftsman looked at the grains in his palm. They were small, thin and mouldy. Some had already sprouted. Some would never grow at all.

"What is the meaning of this?" he asked.

The King's son cackled again. "Why, that's your field of wheat. That's your seven harvests. All you need to do is clear a field and plough it, then sow the grain and wait for it to ripen. Repeat six times and there's your seven harvests!"

And with that he walked, giggling shrilly, out of the workshop.

The Craftsman scattered the grains into his fire. They hissed and flared. The Craftsman called on all the Gods of the earth and sky to give him revenge on this strutting jay-bird who had cheated him. He would not tell the King. He would trust the Gods and bide his time.

*   *   *   *

Seven years passed. The old King grew weak. His eyes grew dim. At last he took to his bed and prepared himself for the day when he would go and live with the Gods. The Craftsman was sad to see his friend so frail. But it made him glad to know that the good King would soon watch over his realm from the high place he had chosen; that his spirit would know the joyful feast that was prepared in the gilded round house of the Sun.

The Craftsman visited his friend every day. He sat by his bed while the old women chanted. They sang songs of the King's good deeds. They sang of the old man's wisdom.

Sometimes the King's darkened eyes seemed to deceive him. He would grasp the Craftsman's hand and call him 'My son'. Then, for a moment, the women paused in their chanting and stared at the Craftsman.

The Craftsman helped to prepare his old friend's last sleeping-place. He dug a shallow oblong pit on a high flat place above the barley fields. This grave was floored with cobbles and lined with flat slabs. The Craftsman carved the story of the King's long life in mystic symbols—circles, spirals, zigzags and snaking lines—on the broad flat flagstone that would cover his old friend's grave.

The King's first son ordered the Craftsman to make a bow and six arrows. With these the King would hunt forever among the stars.

It was a happy-sad sort of work. The Craftsman fashioned six arrowheads as thin as a leaf—perfectly barbed and sharp as a wasp. The arrows were as straight as a sunbeam. The flights were of eagle's feathers. The bow he made was a mighty hunter's weapon, bound with decorative bands.

He brought the bow and arrows to the King's place. It was a cold day and the Craftsman wore a shaggy goatskin coat and hood. He met the King's first son as he entered the royal enclosure.

"I have brought the bow and arrows for your father's hunting in the sky," he said.

The first son scowled and growled. He had on his hunting clothes. His cheeks were streaked with the red paint of his hunting face. His beard was dyed red for hunting. The big bronze axe was slung from his shoulder. He grasped a bronze-bladed spear in his hand.

"Bah!" he exclaimed roughly. "I can't be bothered with that now. I've got better things to do than sit by a half-dead old man. I'm away to hunt the boar in the woods. In any case, the old fool is blind and his mind is wandering. He doesn't even recognise me as his son."

And he pushed past the Craftsman and went to his hunting.

The Craftsman went into the King's house. He placed the bow and the arrows at the King's side. The old man opened his eyes. He raised a hand and stroked the rough goatskin hood and collar of the Craftsman's coat.

"Ah! My strongest boldest son," he murmured. "You bring me a fine bow and arrows for when I shall hunt among the stars. For this day's work you shall be king after me."

At these words the women stopped their chanting. They looked at one another in amazement. The Craftsman was embarrassed. He made his excuses and left.

The King's sly smooth-faced second son came to the Craftsman. He ordered an archer's wrist-guard and six arrows for his father to use when hunting with the Gods.

It was a sad-happy sort of work. The Craftsman fashioned six arrowheads as thin as a fingernail—perfectly barbed and sharp as a bird's eye. The arrows were as straight as a wildcat's stare. The flights were of white swan's feathers. The wrist-guard he made of polished greenstone with four gold studs.

He brought the arrows and the wrist-guard to the King's place. It was a warm day. The Craftsman was dressed neatly in a fine linen shirt with some small beads in his hair. He met the King's younger son as he entered the royal enclosure.

"I have brought the arrows and wrist-guard for your father's hunting with the Gods," he said.

The second son sneered. He was dressed in his finest fringed and tasselled clothes. A pretty slave girl clung gigglingly to each arm. A third girl carried a brimming pot of beer.

"Bah!" he pouted irritably. "I can't be bothered with that now. I've got better things to do than sit by a half-dead old man. These ladies need my company more than he does. In any case the old fool is blind and his mind is wandering. He doesn't even recognise me as his son."

A pretty slave girl clung gigglingly to each arm.

And he pushed past the Craftsman and allowed the giggling girls to lead him towards his own round house.

The Craftsman went into the King's house. He placed the arrows and the wrist-guard at the King's side. The old man opened his eyes. He raised his hand to stroke the soft linen of the Craftsman's shirt and touch the small beads in his friend's hair.

"Ah! My handsome soft son. You bring me fine arrows and a kingly wrist-guard for when I shall hunt among the stars. For this day's work you shall be king after me."

At these words the women stopped their chanting. They looked at one another in amazement. The Craftsman was embarrassed. He made his excuses and left.

That evening under a waning moon, the old King died. As the sun rose next morning the people laid their king in the stone-lined pit. He lay crouched as though asleep, his face towards the midday sun. He was dressed in his finest clothes. Jet buttons gleamed blackly on his coat. A collar of jet beads was fastened upon his breast. His stiff fingers grasped a stone-headed mace. The Gods would know he was a king. A bronze dagger hung at the old King's hip. The greenstone wrist-guard was tied around his left forearm. The bow and twelve arrows were placed ready to hand. At his lips was placed the golden kingly cup, brimming with fresh beer. A joint of pork was laid at his elbow. He would need this food and drink during his long voyage in the silver boat of the Moon.

The Gods would know he was a king.

With tears of joy, the King's two sons dragged the decorated stone slab across to seal their father's grave. Now the King could begin his journey to the stars. With tears of sadness the people began to heap a cairn of stones over their King's sleeping place. From time to time he would descend from the heavens to this high place. From here he would watch over his realm.

But now the valley folk had no king. There was no one with the wisdom of the Gods to give judgement in disputes between neighbours. There was no one to speak with the Gods in the Midsummer circle of great stones. The people grew fearful: like a flock of sheep without a ram; like goats who smell a wolf on the pasture. Only the Craftsman seemed unconcerned. He smiled a knowing smile.

"Who shall be our king?" the fearful people cried.

And then the old women who had chanted in the King's house told of what they had seen. They told how twice the King had said the Craftsman should be king. The King's two sons glared as the Craftsman spoke to the people.

"It is true that I was twice chosen by the King. But perhaps his eyes were dimmed by his old age. Perhaps his mind was clouded by his weariness and pain. Perhaps the Gods did not speak in his words. And because there is doubt, I shall stand aside. I shall stand aside so that the old King's strongest son and the good King's handsomest son may claim their birthright."

"But which shall be our king?" the people cried in confusion. "Tell us, wise Craftsman, which it shall be!" They begged.

"I cannot," said the Craftsman. "It is a choice that only the Gods can make."

"Of course it must be me," bawled the first son. "I shall be king because I am older and stronger."

"No! It must be me," shrieked the younger son. "The Gods love me because I am the handsomest."

"It will be me," growled the first son, wielding his big bronze axe.

"It will be me," snarled the second son, a bronze dagger gleaming in his hand.

The people drew back in horror. Savagely the brothers flew at each other. In a flurry of fists and flashing bronze, as sudden as the fury of robins, the King's sons were locked in a frenzy of blood. They kicked and clawed. The bronze blades slashed and clashed. Then both fell back.

Both brothers staggered. Blood flowed. Both brothers collapsed onto the ground. The people gasped. Three slave girls ran forward to help the younger man. Some burly men ran to the aid of the first son. The people recoiled in horror. The younger son's face was ripped open from his eyebrow to his jaw. It was a terrible wound, pouring with blood. His handsome face was scarred for life. The first son clutched his right hand. Blood gushed onto the ground. Two fingers had been severed. He would never draw a hunter's bow again.

The Craftsman stepped forward.

"The Gods have spoken," he said. "The old King chose me. He chose me twice. He chose me, not in the folly of an old man but with the judgement of a wise man. Now the Gods confirm his choice." The Craftsman pointed scornfully at the King's two sons. "These selfish men were unworthy before. They are more unworthy now. Their jealousy has marred their beauty. Their greed has marred their strength. Neither of these selfish damaged men can be our king."

"Then all the people cried aloud, "The Craftsman shall be king! The Craftsman shall be king! The old King chose him twice! The old King was wise. The Gods confirm the choice! The Craftsman shall be king!"

And so he was.

The old King's sons slunk away in shame and were never seen again. The Craftsman ruled the valley with generosity and wisdom for many years. Each year he greeted the Gods in the Midsummer circle of great stones. He received the wisdom of the Moon three times in his long and happy life. And, at last, he too was laid beneath a tall cairn of stones on the high place above the barley fields. And so the Craftsman sailed in the silver boat of the Moon to join his friend, the good old King, among the stars and to dwell in the round gilded house of the Sun forever.

The silver boat of the Moon

CHAPTER 7

▼

THE GIRL WHO DANCED

In the quiet grey time before dawn, the door of the chief's round house creaked open. An old man stepped out into the chilly half-light. He stepped out to welcome the dawn. It was his duty to greet the goodly Sun on each new day. He welcomed the Sun of Summer, who came from a place beneath the north-eastern hills with scarcely a darkness between the dusk and dawn. He welcomed the Sun of Winter, who rose reluctantly from his rest below the south-east hills when the air was filled with mist and frost. It was a great honour to be a chief and greet the Sun on each new day.

Today the chief pulled his woollen cloak tight around his shoulders. The world was damp with dreary drizzle. Raindrops dripped from the thatched roof of the chief's round house.

The chief was old. His hair was white. But his eyes were bright. And his back was as straight as a spear shaft. His arm was not as strong as it once had been. He did not often now draw a bow. But his hand was steady. And his thoughts were as keen as the bright bronze edge of a knife.

The chief walked quickly. He threaded his way among the round houses of the sleeping village. He passed through the gateway in the stone wall that encircled his village. He took the path that led up hill through the neat rectangular fields.

He paused in a grassy space. A great pale stone swelled from the earth like the cool haunch of a sleeping woman. The flanks of the whitestone were carved with patterns of rings and dots and curving lines. The designs had been pecked out with a hardstone point by people of the long long-ago time. The patterns had magic meanings. Nobody now remembered the tales they told. But the magic remained.

"Bless this new day good mother," sang the old chief. "Make the corn grow high. Make your daughters strong."

He tossed a handful of barley flour in the air for an offering. It blew like smoke on the breeze. It fell like frost on the grass.

"Bless this new day good mother," sang the old chief.

The sky lightened as the chief walked onto the pasture. Raindrops sparkled on his frost-white hair. The chief passed the grey stone house that hunched from the green grass. He turned his face away. Evil came to men whose eyes lingered on the grey stone house. It belonged to the race of giants who had lived long long ago—when the world was filled with spirits and ruled by the magic of women. But the Sun and Stars and the salt-white Moon—the gods and goddesses of the light—had shrivelled the giants and sealed their women's magic in the big stone house. But still, now and then, a spiteful sprite wormed its way through the blocked doorway to make mischief and misery in the world.

A little way from the grey stone house with its rubbly weed-grown roof and tumble-down leaning walls, stood a singly stately guardian. The stone reared twice as tall as the tallest man—slender, pointed, gracefully bowed and gently leaning. A broad sash of magic whitestone slanted from shoulder to hip across the breast of Father-of-Stone.

The chief stood close to the source of men's power in the world. He clasped Father-of-Stone in his arms. He rested his cheek upon the white sash as he had done every day for more than fifty years. And, as every day for more than fifty years, his old bones grew stiff and strong with the strength of the stone.

Now the chief was ready to enter the great circle of the Sun. He passed through the gateway in the circling stony bank. He crossed the narrow path that spanned the ring of ditch. He stood at the centre of the round of dancing stones. Each stone was a spirit with the life of countless generations. Tall or fat, rugged or graceful, hunched or slender, stately or coy—each stone in the ring had a name and a history. Every stone was alive.

A sheep had strayed into the great circle during the night. It stared at the man, grass in mouth. The chief chased the silly creature away. It clattered complaining into the weedy ditch. It scampered up and over the encircling bank. This was a bad sign. The gods would be angry. In the old days the sheep would have been killed—an offering to the gods. And its owner would have been punished for invading this special place. But things were different now. People did not respect the gods as once they did.

The chief stood, arms outstretched. He stood in the rain as the sky brightened in the east. He welcomed the day. And a waterish Sun clambered heavily from beneath the far hills. He shone feebly in the damp distance. Rain fell steadily.

His duty done, the chief returned home. The village was stirring now. Sticks snapped and pots chinked in the round houses as the women made up their fires and prepared breakfast. Girls passed carrying heavy water pots. Men and boys were setting off for their work in the fields or on the pasture.

Older folk bowed deeply as their chief passed. But younger folk merely nodded. Some ignored him altogether. The chief sighed. Respect for elders—respect for the old ways—was fading fast in the long ago time.

The chief returned to his own round house. It stood within a stone walled enclosure. In the old days the chief's house was the largest in the village. But times had changed. Several villagers—men with many cattle, many wives and many strong sons—had built houses that were larger than the chief's. Their tall conical roofs overshadowed the houses of their neighbours, servants and slaves. And the thatch was fresh and watertight—unlike the mouldy, mossy leaky roof of the chief's modest home.

The largest house in the village belonged to the priest of the Goddess. He was a cunning, cruel, sly-eyed man. He did not respect the gods of the sky. He did not respect the chief. But he was admired by the younger men of the village. He was adored by their wives and daughters. He was feared, too, because he heard the whispered voice of the Goddess.

The chief did not understand the Goddess. In the olden days men had worshipped the gods of the sky and been happy. The goodly Sun shone every day. The Moon smiled in the night sky. And all was well. But now the Sun sulked in a cloak of clouds. The nights were dark. And the valley bottom—where once there had been green meadows and bright springs where jolly water sprites played— was now choked with dank woodland. The trees in the valley shaded a secret dark and boggy pool. This was where the Goddess lived.

The Goddess was not like the goodly open-hearted Sun or the clean-faced Moon. She was not generous like the white Mothering-Stone of the fields. She was not strong and honest like Father-of-Stone. She was dark and mysterious. Nobody saw her. No one could look into her haggish eyes and hope to live. She was feared. She was worshipped where she lurked in the waters of a peat-black pool—beneath tangled trees that dripped with moss and lichen—strangled by ivy and poisonous mistletoe.

The chief had been to the pool of the Goddess only once. It was a fearful place. Around the pool stood strange-shaped stumps of wood. Mouldy and moss-clad they seemed like images of men and women—but changed and twisted with evil magic. The chief had gazed into the water. He saw a glint like gold or bright bronze: rich offerings—bangles, neck-rings, axes and spearheads—flung into the waters by the people of the Goddess when they begged her for a blessing. A ripple in the water made the chief start back in terror. The Goddess was no respecter of chiefs.

The pool of the Goddess

Now the chief entered his own small house. His granddaughter squatted at the fireside preparing breakfast. The girl's movements were as quick and pretty as the flight of a butterfly. She sang a merry song. Her voice brightened the smoky air of the chief's small house.

The girl was called Dancing-Girl. She was the chief's whole hope and joy. She was the daughter of his only son, who had fallen in love with a slave girl and married her. Of course, the chief had disapproved. But the slave woman's gentleness had melted disapproval into love. So he had at last embraced her—no longer a slave—as his own dear daughter. But now both son and daughter were dead. They died in the year when late frosts killed the corn. Hunger came to the village. After the frost came the rain. The rains brought sickness to the village. And the sickness carried away the soft wife of the chief's only son. Then the upland folk had come. They were starving. They begged for food, but there was none to spare. They departed, angry and disappointed. They returned with axes and spears. Now they demanded food. But there was none to give. There was fighting and terrible slaughter. And when the uplanders at last were driven away, the chief's son was dead and his baby granddaughter an orphan.

Now the village mistrusted strangers. A wall was built around the houses. And the men all carried axes and spears—even when they went to work among the fields or to tend their cattle on the pasture. Rich men carried bright bronze swords.

"Grandfather!" the girl exclaimed as the chief closed the door behind him. "You are cold and wet!"

She leaped across the fire, scattering sparky spirits in the smoky air. She helped her grandfather with the pins of his cloak. She cast a fleece around his shoulders and led him to his stool at the fireside. She brought him breakfast on a chiefly dish. There was bread and honey, salty smoky bacon, creamy cheese and pale butter. The girl placed a bowl of warm milk in her grandfather's hand. The chief kissed his granddaughter. And for a moment he thought it might be better to be an ordinary old man with a loving child than the greatest chief in all the world.

As he finished his meal, there was a knock at the door. Dancing-Girl sprang up and skipped to open it. In the doorway, with the thatch pattering raindrops on the hood of his cloak, stood the priest of the Goddess. He came to the fireside. He bowed very low to the chief. But it was a sneering bow that showed no respect. Dancing-Girl stood behind her grandfather. Girls must be silent while men are speaking.

... it was a sneering bow that showed no respect.

"I come to you, Oh chief, on behalf of the Goddess—whose humble servant I am."

"The servant is welcome in my house," replied the chief stiffly. He gestured for the visitor to be seated.

"Oh great chief, the servant of the Goddess thanks you for allowing him to sit at your noble fireside."

The priest's words were humble, but his eyes were not. He glanced slyly around the chief's house. He smirked. His own house was much larger than the chief's. And it was better furnished too—with furs and woven hangings, fine pottery, bright bronze and gold. He had slaves too, and wives and strong sons. The old chief had only one granddaughter beneath his leaky roof—and she was the child of a slave.

"I come humbly to the great house of my chief to beg a favour—on behalf of the people of the Goddess."

The chief said nothing. There was an awkward silence.

"The people of the Goddess beg your blessing on their Midsummer worship."

The chief spoke slowly and with dignity. "I cannot give a blessing. Only the gods can give blessings. And at Midsummer the gods will give their blessing as always, in the great circle of the Sun."

"Oh chief, we all know how you love the old gods of the sky. We thank you for your devotion on our behalf. But there are other deities who must be served."

The chief said nothing.

"The Goddess must be served."

The chief made no movement to show he agreed.

"The people demand that the Goddess is honoured."

"The people cannot demand from a chief," said the chief crossly.

"Oh no, great chief," replied the priest hastily. "Do not misunderstand me. I am just an ordinary man. I do not have the gift of words. What I mean to say is that the Goddess demands and her people request—they request very humbly."

"The people are like children." The chief was scornful. "Your Goddess demands, but what does she give in return? Your people sacrifice their best beasts. They place fine bronze—and gold too—in her dark pool. But she gives them nothing. It seems to me that the only person the Goddess rewards is her priest— who has more cattle and bronze and slaves and wives than anyone else in the village." The chief's wise eye twinkled. "I wonder why that is?"

The priest's eyes flashed with anger. His hand gripped the hilt of his sword. Then the cloak of humbleness fell again upon him. "Oh chief, it is true the Goddess blesses me. She blesses me far above what I deserve. But who can know why the gods favour one man …" his sly eyes glanced around the chief's shabby home "… and not another?"

"If the people would honour the good old gods of their grandfathers—then all would be favoured. All would be well."

"The old gods! Bah!" exclaimed the priest. "The old gods are weak and worn out. The Sun is feeble. The Moon hides in clouds. The world is changing. The Goddess of the pool is the new power in the world. The people know that, even if their chief does not. The people look to the future. They do not live in the past."

"Perhaps it is so. Or perhaps the Sun is wrapped in a cloak of rain because he is sad that our people turn from him to other gods. But I will not argue with you. Tell me what you want."

"I want nothing for myself. But the Goddess has her needs."

"And what does your goddess want from me?"

A wicked glint appeared in the priest's eye. "The Goddess wants … your granddaughter."

The chief was astonished. Anger flared in his heart. The priest saw it. He wrung his hands in his humblest manner.

"Oh do not misunderstand me, great chief! Do not be angry because I have not words of wisdom to speak what I mean. The people ask—they humbly beg—their great chief to permit his pretty daughter to dance for them; just to dance for one short day to honour the Goddess of the pool."

At this young Dancing-Girl clapped her hands with delight. "Oh grandfather!" she exclaimed. "Oh, do say yes. I love to dance. I would so like to dance for the people and their goddess."

But the chief frowned. A girl should not interrupt men's talk. He did not love the Goddess of the pool. And he did not trust the priest. He thought for a moment. Then he spoke.

"But you have three daughters of your own. Can they not dance?"

"Oh yes! But not so well as your granddaughter. She dances like a spirit of air. And she has the blood of kings in her veins. Her dancing would bring great honour to our celebrations."

The chief spoke solemnly. "The best dancer would bring the greatest honour. We must be sure the best dancer is chosen."

"But young Dancing-Girl is the best dancer in the village!" the priest protested.

And the chief knew it was true. Nonetheless he spoke solemnly in his chiefly judgement voice.

"There shall be a competition," he said. "In seven days time, at Father-of-Stone, your daughters and my granddaughter shall dance together. Father-of-Stone shall judge who dances best—and decide who shall dance for your goddess."

The priest began to protest. This was not what he wanted. But the chief, with a wave of his hand, indicated that the interview was over. The priest rose. He bowed a shallow angry bow and marched from the house. The door slammed shut.

Dancing-Girl kissed her grandfather. "I am sorry I interrupted the men's talk," she said. "Please do not be angry."

The chief smiled. "I am not angry. I could not be angry with you. But I am angry with that … that … that so-called priest. He is wicked and deceitful. And his goddess is hungry and cruel."

"But he only wants me to dance."

The chief stroked his granddaughter's hair. "That is what he said. But I do not trust the man. I do not trust his cruel goddess"

"But the competition—and good Father-of-Stone—will decide who shall dance." A cloud passed across the girl's face. "Or do you wish I should lose the contest on purpose—dance badly so the priest's daughters are chosen? I will dance badly if you wish."

"No. That will not do. That would bring dishonour on you and on this house. And anyway, the priest is not so easily deceived. He is wicked but he is clever too. No, you must dance your very best. Father-of-Stone will decide who shall win the competition. And we must trust the wisdom of the good old gods."

Later that day the chief went to the village craftsman. He took with him a bag containing his most precious possessions—a gold neck-ring, a festoon of honey-bright yellow amber, and a dozen night-shining black jet buttons. When he returned the bag was empty, but there was a satisfied smile on the wise chief's lips.

The day of the dancing competition came at last. The men, women and children—even the slaves—formed a circle of excited chatter around tall Father-of-Stone. The chief was dressed with sombre dignity in his every-day clothes. The priest glittered with gold and green-glass beads. His bronze sword gleamed like polished sunshine. Chief and priest bowed to the stone. They bowed stiffly to each other.

Four dancing girls came from the crowd—the priest's three bonny daughters and the chief's precious granddaughter. They seemed like barefoot sprites escaped from some happy place to bring a moment of delight to the world of men. They wore short tasselled skirts, fastened with fancy belts, each hung with a shining bronze disk to honour the Sun. Glittering bangles clinked and jingled on their arms and ankles. Gleaming gold rings hung from their ears and circled their slender necks.

The chief stepped forward. The crowd hushed. He spoke to his people.

"This day we ask good Father-of-Stone to judge the dancing of our daughters. The girl who dances best today will dance at Midsummer for the Goddess of the pool." The chief smiled his knowing smile. "But before the contest begins, I have a gift for each girl who dances."

The chief drew a bundle from beneath his cloak. He unwrapped it to reveal four pairs of delicate dancing sandals. All were made of the softest leather and sewn with the finest stitching. One pair was decorated with leaf-thin bands of gold. A second sparkled with honey-bright amber. The third was studded with night-shining jet. One pair of sandals was plain and undecorated.

"Come girls," the chief beckoned. "You may each choose the shoes you would like to dance in."

The priest's daughters squealed with delight and rushed forward. They pushed little Dancing-Girl aside. They forgot to curtsey to the chief. They snatched the gilded and beaded sandals from his hands. Dancing-Girl curtseyed respectfully to her grandfather. He placed the plain leather sandals in her hands.

But the priest was suspicious. What trick was this? He carefully examined each of the decorated sandals. He sniffed them in case there was magic in their stitching. At last he allowed his girls to put on their gorgeous dancing-shoes. Young Dancing-Girl carefully fastened her soft plain sandals.

And now the dancing began. Flutes trilled to the beat of a dozen drums and the hiss of as many rattles. Horns brayed and boomed. Bronze bells and tambourines tinkled. And the four girls danced.

The four girls danced around Father-of-Stone who swayed, it seemed, approvingly in time to the music. The four girls' footsteps were as airy as the flight of the mayfly—leaping, jumping, nimbly tripping; tumbling, prancing, gaily skipping; bounding, spinning, lightly flitting. The girls sprang in the air—each higher than the other. They tumbled in quick slick handsprings—as carefree and on their hands as on their feet. They danced for the people. They danced for Father-of-Stone. They danced for joy.

The girls danced. The drums beat a dizzying rhythm. The girls danced. The horns boomed and brayed. The girls danced. Bronze bells jingled and clashed. And the girls danced.

But suddenly little Dancing-Girl was limping. She danced so that she favoured one foot. She leaped in the air, but landed awkwardly. She sprang on her hands. But landing back on her feet she cried out with pain. Once she staggered. Once she almost fell. Her limping steps were clumsy, ugly. The people cried out, "The chief's girl is crippled!" They mocked her awkwardness. "The chief's slave-child cannot dance," they jeered.

Dancing-Girl heard their words. She was angry and ashamed. She knew that she was the best dancer. But inside the dancing sandal her foot burned like fire. She stumbled. Tears came to her eyes. Tears came because of the pain. And tears of shame came, because she danced badly and the people called her slave-girl. Then she stumbled and fell.

Through the haze of tears and music, pain and shame, she heard the peoples' howl of mocking laughter. "Slave-girl! Limping-dancer! Cripple-child!"

"The chief's slave-child cannot dance," they jeered.

But the dance went on. The priest's three bonny daughters still danced. The music in their heads and in their feet cast a dancing spell. The priest cried out for them to stop. But they heard only the music. He waved his arms to make his girls stop. But they saw only the flashing bangles and the sparkling shoes and the sky above and the ground beneath.

At last the priest's two youngest daughters began to tire. Their dancing grew ragged. Now and then they lost the rhythm of the music. Now and then they faltered in their leaping steps. At last they slumped to the ground, weary and faint, panting for breath. Only the priest's handsome eldest daughter remained on her feet.

And the people all cried, "The priest's eldest daughter wins! The priest's handsome daughter is our dancer! The priest's pretty girl will dance for the Goddess of the pool!"

The crowd dispersed. The priest scowled as he shepherded his daughters home. The girls, poor things, did not know why their father was so angry. They did not know he had wanted the chief's girl to win. Because he feared what the cruel jealous Goddess might do when she saw a pretty girl dancing at her poolside. But he dared not disappoint the people of the Goddess. Though he was their priest, he was also in their power. Now the people wanted his daughter to dance. And so dance she must.

When the people were gone, the chief bowed solemnly to Father-of-Stone. Then he went to his granddaughter. She lay huddled on the ground. "I have shamed you," she sobbed. "I am just a clumsy slave-child."

Tenderly the old man helped the girl to sit up. He dried her tears. He gently unfastened her sandals. The girl's foot was bleeding. With a sly grin the chief examined the bloodstained sandal. Carefully he drew a tiny sharp bronze pin from the sole. He held it so it glittered in the light.

Now the girl understood. The wise chief knew that the greedy daughters of the wicked priest would seize the finest shoes for themselves. But he knew too that nothing would prevent his own proud dancing girl from dancing her very best. And so he had placed the sharp pin in the heel of the plain sandal. Dancing-Girl had lost the contest so that the chief could win a victory over the priest. Beaming triumphantly, he helped his granddaughter home.

*   *   *   *

And today it is the Midsummer morn. This is the grey time before the dawn. The air is damp with dreary drizzle. The sky is heavy with cloud.

The old chief stands in the Midsummer circle of great stones. He wears a thin golden neck-ring. Six jet buttons gleam blackly on his jacket. Small gold ornaments glister in his hair. Bronze bangles chink on his arms and ankles. In his hand he carries the blackstone axe-hammer of kingship that has been handed down from father to son since the time of the first kings. An old-fashioned bronze axe, polished like gold, hangs at his hip.

Somewhere far away—far below the circle of the Sun—another ceremony takes place. A handsome girl dances beside a pool of black water. She dances in a mossy place of dank trees all strangled with ivy and mistletoe. She dances among the mouldy stumpish idols while the people of the Goddess fling offerings—fine bronze tools and weapons—to the hag of the black water. They place pots of ale and milk at the waterside. They sprinkle the blood of animals into the peat-black pool. They beat their drums. They shout in a frenzy. The goddess is hungry. The goddess is always hungry.

Meanwhile, in the circle of the Sun a pretty girl dances. It is Dancing-Girl. She wears a tasselled skirt with a fancy belt and a disk of bronze, a shiny neck-ring, earrings of gold, and bangles of bronze. Her foot is healed. She dances barefoot, sunwise around the high circling bank. She dances into the ring of stones. Her dance weaves in and out among the circling stones. She is the best dancer in the world. She dances round each stone sunwise. She dances round each stone—tall and fat, rugged and graceful, hunched and slender, stately and coy. She calls each stone by name—Father-of-Wisdom, Mother-of-Life, Mighty-Hunter, Healer, Dream-Giver, Mischief-Maker, Maiden, Wise-King, Child-of-Light.

She dances to the sunrise side of the circle as the goodly Sun peers from behind the grey and faraway hills. And suddenly his Midsummer waking burns away the clouds that hide the sky. A dazzle of light floods the great circle. Sunshine and shadow dance among the ringing stones. The dancing girl cries out for joy. She leaps and skips and tumbles for the delight of the goodly Sun. The chief's gold and bronze gleam like the glory of kings in the olden times. And the chief smiles as if meeting an old friend after a long separation.

Later the old chief walks home. He holds the small hand of Dancing-Girl. The old man and the girl are happy. The gods are pleased.

"The goodly Sun showed his face to us in the Midsummer circle today," says the girl.

"He showed his face as in the olden days," murmurs the old chief contentedly.

"Does that mean the rains will stop and the sky become blue again—like in the olden days?"

"Perhaps."

"So now will the goodly Sun show his power as in the olden days? Will he make the cruel Goddess wither away? Will all be well—as it was before the rains came?" the girl asks anxiously.

But her grandfather's thoughts are far away. He gazes sadly down towards the valley bottom where woodland shrouds the dark pool of the Goddess. Strange and savage cries drift from the trees. The hungry Goddess is devouring the food that her people bring.

"Perhaps it does not matter whether the Sun shines," muses the chief at last. "And perhaps it does not even matter which gods we follow: the goodly Sun or the hungry Goddess of the pool—or some other god whose name we do not yet know. Perhaps it does not matter which god we follow, so long as we are kind to one another. If there is respect for wisdom—and if there is love in the world—then all will be well."

And so it was.

… then all will be well.

ABOUT THE AUTHOR

John Barrett is an archivist, historian and cyclist. Christine Clerk is a mathematician, physicist, artist—and cyclist. Together, as author and illustrator, they have enjoyed a lifetime of involvement in exploring, recording and researching the historic landscapes, sites, monuments and documentary heritage of Northeast Scotland.

John Barrett has published poetry and literary criticism as well as numerous articles on archives and aspects of local history from the Stone Age to the twentieth century. He is co-author of books on local history, palaeography, genealogy and domestic architecture—all illustrated by Christine Clerk. He has also written an episodic history of the Royal Burgh of Forres and is co-author of a children's adventure in family history—gorgeously illustrated by Christine Clerk.

John Barrett's first novel for children, titled *The Salt Trader's Boy*, was published in 2003. This story is set in the strange, dangerous and magical world of the New Stone Age, six thousand years ago. The (pre)historical background to the novel—and Christine Clerk's illustrations—drew upon extensive travel and research into Neolithic societies, sites and monuments in Scotland and the wider European culture zone of Britain and Ireland, The Netherlands, Denmark, France and The Mediterranean.

In 2004 John Barrett published an academic edition of a seminal volume of seventeenth-century memoirs under the title *Mr James Allan: the journey of a lifetime*. A historical novel, for older children and young adults, titled *Broken Sword*, was inspired by Mr James Allan. This adventure, set within the religious and political turmoil of seventeenth century Scotland, will be published shortly. Meanwhile John Barrett is collaborating on an academic study of northeast Scotland during the age of the Covenants.

A short story for children, *The Kindness of Strangers* (the third tale of the *Whitestone* suite), was runner-up in the Eildon Tree Competition 2005.

The Whitestone Stories draw upon extensive academic research to introduce prehistoric societies, from the Mesolithic to the Bronze Age, to younger children—and to the older brothers and sisters, parents and teachers who will read the stories to them.

978-0-595-42435-1
0-595-42435-X

Printed in the United Kingdom
by Lightning Source UK Ltd.
120938UK00002B/181-240